The Re

By M:

GW00375311

Copyright © 2016 by Mark Warren

All rights reserved. No part of this publication may be reproduced, distributed, or transmitted in any form or by any means, including photocopying, recording, or other electronic or mechanical methods, without the prior written permission of the publisher, except in the case of brief quotations embodied in critical reviews and certain other non commercial uses permitted by copyright law.

For Kate, Chloe, Georgia, Mum, Dad, Sue, Barry and Kat – without all of your support this book would have remained a dream.

Contents

Bulletproof

It was the morning after the storm in suburbia. Sleep had not been forthcoming thanks largely to the persistent rattling of a rogue can in the garden. I had discounted the notion of clambering out of the bed and venturing outside to end its quest across the patio. The effort involved in doing so would have woken me completely and therefore rendered the exercise counter-productive. So instead I had convinced myself the better option was to try and sleep while Mother Nature relentlessly attempted to separate the roof tiles from the rest of the house and fill it with rainwater. Hindsight was a wonderful thing and the reality of the situation was that I spent the night half awake and half asleep. Of course the minute I eventually drifted into some form of meaningful sleep the alarm clock had sounded and I realised a long and weary day beckoned.

'Dad, the fence has come down!' cried Ellen as she burst into our bedroom with all the finesse of a charging rhinoceros. If there was one thing worse than a nine year old that didn't knock it was being presented with bad news by that person.

'Okay I'll get Richard Long to sort it out, thanks' I replied without giving it a second thought. After all, I had enjoyed a good month in terms of commission and some pipeline deals had begun to bear the fruits of my labour. As a general rule if something went wrong in my world I would pay someone to fix it. After years of hard graft for the same company I felt the right had been earned to adopt such an approach. The fact that I possessed the DIY skills of a halibut could have been classed as another crucial factor.

'Is anyone in the bathroom?' I asked Ellen hopefully.

'It was empty a minute ago Daddy' she replied as she left the room. I clambered out of bed and caught sight of myself in the mirror which was never a pleasant experience. It served as an unwanted reminder that my body had begun to withdraw the supply of hair to my scalp and chosen to re-distribute it to other less desirable areas. I assumed this was standard procedure for a man in his early forties.

I made my way onto the landing and to my relief the bathroom door had indeed been left ajar. The monkey chattering in my brain had already begun - I usually started obsessing about work long before I even made it to the car, let alone the office. I grabbed a towel then wandered into the bathroom and noticed the rays of sunlight forcing their way through the venetian blinds that exposed a plethora of floating dust particles. Why was it always sunny after a storm, I pondered? Whilst locking the door I thought it wise to address the fact my bladder felt like it was on the verge of rupturing. Much like smoking, the first one of the day was always the best. I undertook the daily challenge of trying to dislodge the toilet freshener with the flow - I had yet to experience any success but the challenge aspect appealed to me. For a bit of variety I would occasionally see how far back I could stand and still reach the toilet. If Rachel had any idea of this ritual she wouldn't have been impressed in the slightest.

'Did you hear that storm last night?' enquired a voice from my right. To my absolute horror Ellen's grandmother Irene languished in the bath, I had obviously been so tired her presence in the room hadn't registered. Thankfully the bubbles obscured the worst bits, on the flip side she had just witnessed one of the small pleasures I derived from my morning routine.

'You remind me of my Bernard he used to have one of those-'

'I think you forgot to lock the door again' I interjected before she could elaborate further as the last thing I needed was a comparison to any part of her deceased husband's anatomy. I was beginning to think we'd made a catastrophic error of judgement agreeing to allow Rachel's mother to move in while her residential home underwent refurbishment. Sadly her general state of confusion had become progressively worse over time and this sort of event was starting to increase in frequency. She often lived in the past and occasionally visited the present – this in addition to a time that never seemed to have existed. The residential home had explained there simply wasn't an available room at any of their sister homes for Irene during the renovation programme. I was beginning to see why. It had come to our attention they regarded her as one of their most cantankerous and tempestuous residents. One might add the word incontinent to that list. As usual I had agreed to let her stay with us in a vain attempt to do the right thing. This had of course backfired on occasion primarily due to her habit of making unhelpful observations at the most inopportune moments. It was either that or her attempts to destroy the house with her random acts of lunacy such as cooking bacon in the toaster. Sometimes it felt like she was deliberately attempting to wreck my marriage to Rachel and I couldn't wait for her to return to her rightful place at Woodford Residential Home. For all that, Ellen loved having her Grandmother under the same roof and if nothing else they kept each other occupied at times.

I left Irene to her own devices in the bath and ambled downstairs. The postman had managed to create an impressive new record in his attempts to throw the post as far down the hall as possible. Scooping up the array of junk mail I walked through to the lounge where the television had been left on for the attention of the invisible man. I switched over to the news channel and a less than sanguine character

11

was busy spreading yet more doom and gloom about the recession to the watching world. He prophesised that this year would be even worse than the previous one and that the economic downturn showed no sign of abating. To be honest I felt fortunate to be one of the few proud owners of a 'job for life' as my boss had recently put it. Having escalated through the ranks within the company over the last nineteen years I had managed to carve out a rewarding career. This had afforded my family a comfortable lifestyle and a respectable detached house within the leafy confines of the commuter belt. Each day the suburban economy lived and breathed and I felt very much a vital organ within it -or at the very least an unseen micro-organism that provided a useful contribution. The media seemed determined to keep the recession going at all costs. Sometimes I wondered if there was one at all or if the whole thing had been fabricated to sell newspapers. Their constant peddling of negative filth had created a self perpetuating cycle of misery that convinced employers and consumers alike that they needed to trim their expenditure. According to reports one of the county's largest banks was on the brink of collapse. This hardly seemed possible considering the exorbitant fees they charged consumers for exceeding their limit by the narrowest of margins. The news feature moved onto another staid man who claimed to be an economist, he spoke of inflation and other such matters that I barely understood. I wondered if the pre-requisite for such a role was that candidates must be over sixty years of age and possess the ability to communicate in a way that the working class would never comprehend. Whilst I pondered such matters over breakfast I lost track of the time until Ellen announced she was leaving for school. There was nothing else for it — I could either indulge in a wet-wipe shower or suffer a day at work tired and unwashed. Maybe the boss would think I had become destitute and offer me a substantial pay rise to spend on a new flat and lots of cheap Scandinavian furniture that would ultimately collapse in twelve months time. Or maybe he would retract his "job for life" statement and send me packing like an unwanted puppy after Christmas.

After breakfast and a hurried attempt at dressing for work Rachel appeared just as I was about to leave the house. She was clearly still half asleep and with her dishevelled hair resembled an alien life form that originated from a previously undiscovered planet.

'Shouldn't you have left by now Tim?' she croaked. She had clearly deduced that I was edging towards lateness and felt the need to further delay me by pointing out the obvious. If there was one thing that irritated me it was someone interrupting my progress to highlight the fact I hadn't completed the very task they were now delaying.

'Yes I must hit the road, Mad Dog will skewer my genitals otherwise' I replied.

'I'm going to the travel agents later, we all need a holiday and Serena said they have a promotion on. Did you have a look at that site?'

I sensed we were entering into that familiar game whereby I had to choose between arriving at work on time and talking about any random subject of Rachel's choice. This had been a feature of our marriage for many years. The thought occurred that she'd had all of the previous evening to discuss such matters but had barely spoken to me. Then the very minute I needed to leave for work she would try and engage me in conversation. Sadly only one of the possible choices open to me actively contributed towards the mortgage.

'I did have a quick look, maybe we could decide later – I really must go now'. The second part of that statement was true therefore it wasn't a complete lie.

'Okay I'm going back to bed, see if I can sleep this headache off' she replied before sauntering off in the direction of the bedroom.

With that I quickly gathered my things and darted out of the front door, ready to do battle with the forces of the business world whilst contemplating what it must be like to have the option of sleeping off a headache. The notion seemed very much like a luxury to me. Nonetheless it was just another day in the world of Tim Fellows and if the truth be told I liked the comfort afforded by my secure job despite the paradox that was my family life. It was fair to say I knew exactly who I was and where I was going – there was something to be said for that. Our neighbour Colin had emerged from his front door at the same time as me and I tried to avoid eye contact. Conversations were never quick with him and I couldn't afford any further delays.

'Morning Tim - has your fence fallen down?' he enquired in keeping with the 'stating the obvious' theme. Why did people feel the need to ask such questions? I suspected what he really wanted to know was how quickly I intended to repair it.

'Yes apparently so, more expense!' I replied quickly jumping into the car before he could comment further.

Although work was situated a few miles from home it seemed today as if it might as well have been in another country. As often happened when running late the traffic gods sensed this and placed obstacles in my path. I could visualise them surveying the playing board and wryly chuckling amongst themselves as they created yet another ridiculous hurdle. Every single traffic light I encountered was red – the conspiracy continued as word spread amongst the traffic light community that Tim Fellows was in a hurry. Another feature of my blighted journey had been the obligatory slow drivers that would let all and sundry exit junctions despite it not being their right of way. I looked forward to my retirement when I planned to exact revenge by deliberately leaving the house every day just before rush hour with the sole intention of clogging up the roads. would perform extraordinary acts of generosity along the way and smile to myself as I basked in the resultant warm fuzzy feeling from such philanthropy. Lunchtimes would be spent in banks and post offices as I attempted to bring each establishment to a grinding halt with complex queries and pretending not to understand anything. This would ensure maximum disruption to the working world, who only had a finite amount of time to complete their tasks.

As I finally approached the building I took a moment to recall my first day there. An older man named Brian had greeted me in the main reception - he closely resembled a frog and wore his trousers as high as humanly possible without forcing a testicle back into his body. In those days I had nothing to offer except raw potential and enthusiasm, which as it turned out was more than a lot of the employees on the payroll. Brian had subsequently left the company a short time after my induction and they didn't even replace him. He did however tell me an interesting story about a man who spent all day just staring out of the window. When a colleague questioned why this person was being paid to do this it transpired he had thought of an idea that had made the company a substantial amount of money whilst looking out of that very pane of glass. I wasn't sure if that was actually true but I found it inspiring all the same. Somehow I didn't think Mad Dog would invest the same faith in me if I adopted this approach. The company had changed a lot since I'd started there and this was driven by a constant hunger to 're-invent' and 'restructure' for the sake of making certain people's CV's look like they had actually achieved something. In my considered view there were two types of people in the workplace – those who did the work and those who talked about it. I had always been a doer which suited me fine but my path to success had often been blighted by those that professed to know better than me. Graduates would come in fresh from university armed with an array of buzz words and statistics but absolutely no common sense or experience. Despite this I had worked my way up the career ladder and became a top performing regional sales manager, responsible for ensuring our national sales targets were met. I was born for this role and thrived on the daily challenges it presented, whilst also becoming a recognised expert in the Paradox system. The latter had helped me create an insurance policy that made me invaluable to the company and I genuinely wondered how my colleagues would ever cope if I left. Of course like all companies the place had its nuances and quirks but it could be argued these very things were also factors that set it apart from other places of work.

As I stepped out of my shiny company car I noticed an object on the floor out of the corner of my bloodshot eye. It was a headless bird. So whatever the day ahead had planned for me it was surely going to be better than this dead starling's. Unless of course you took the view that his day couldn't get any worse, whereas potentially mine could well do. Brushing aside this surprisingly negative thought I breezed into the reception. Mary the receptionist was busy watching the plasma TV that was meant for visitors and gave me a cursory glance before emitting a sarcastic 'Afternoon Tim'. At that moment in my haste I collided with a burly IT developer called Rob, he was a mountain of a man who lived alone with nobody but his pet reptile for company. The pair of them spent many a romantic evening parked on his hideous green corner sofa, watching his favourite martial art movies. We pretended to square up to each other in mock anger.

'If you were my size...' I quipped. He chuckled at the exchange as he towered over me.

'I'd be under developed' he countered before lumbering off down the corridor like Frankenstein's monster. That riposte was certainly high on the list of his better comebacks.

The issue I had with being late on a Monday was the walk of shame that had to be endured as you approached the glass meeting room known colloquially as the Goldfish Bowl. Every Monday we'd have the sales conference call where people from our other branches dialled in and tried to gain kudos by pretending they were winning untold amounts of new business. From where our new boss, known as Mad Dog, sat he was able to fix you in a psychotic stare as you approached the Bowl. That five second walk could feel like hours sometimes. I tried to slip in the door quietly whilst mouthing the word 'sorry' but the door handle entered into my suit jacket sleeve and I inadvertently kicked the door and then stumbled into the room. Mad Dog and the others stopped in the middle of their telephone debate and stared at me as if I was some sort of buffoon. At that moment the starling was definitely having a better time of things and I hoped this wasn't a marker for the kind of day that lay ahead.

Goldfish

The day had thankfully improved after its shaky beginnings. Mad Dog had seemingly forgiven me for my lateness and was busy barking orders and snarling at the rest of the sales force. I had realised some time ago that he was one of those curious people that had a propensity towards occasional eruptions of anger, which would then subside as quickly as they started and in his mind it was all over. By stark contrast it seemed I would stew on matters for days and sometimes weeks if something had irked me. I could recall many occasions where he had berated me and then moved on instantly whilst I lost sleep over it in the ensuing days.

Glancing out of the window and even from this distance I could make out the form of the starling corpse next to the car. At that moment Mad Dog picked up the phone and proceeded to speak at such an incredibly low tone I couldn't believe the person on the other end would be able to hear him. His whole body language had shifted noticeably as he hunched over the desk with a look that could otherwise be mistaken for constipation. From my personal experience any attempt to lower my voice resulted in the recipient requiring you to raise your voice to a louder volume than normal to compensate for the initial confusion caused by being too quiet. Yet he seemed to have honed the skill to a fine art. Presumably a deal had fallen out of bed and he was about to break the news to us in his own inimitable style. All three of us had noticed the mysterious call and continued to impersonate busy workers whilst covertly eavesdropping. The main purpose was to gain intelligence that could be shared via online messaging. This practice had become a side-sport that served to brighten up our days - we constantly looked to obtain that killer piece of intelligence and then be the first to break the news to the others. On this occasion though, it wasn't to be. He finished the call and for the first time since I'd known him looked visibly shaken.

'Is everything okay?' I offered. I really didn't know why people asked that when things clearly weren't okay but in the absence of any better ideas it was the best I could do.

'The Lord works in mysterious ways but the devil even more so' came the reply as he hauled his slightly overweight frame out of his leather chair and headed for the door. He could be annoyingly cryptic at times, did he not realise how it could affect productivity? We then had to devote extra time to de-cipher his latest lament amongst ourselves. We looked at each other and systematically shrugged our shoulders as nobody was able to hazard a guess. He had looked ashen faced as he walked out of the room. One thing was for sure - whatever the content of that call it didn't appear to be good news

It was some while before he re-appeared by which time we had resigned ourselves to the fact it was a 'need to know' situation – put simply we needed to know. I had spent my lunch hour trying to make contact with Richard Long in order that he could repair the fence before the local foxes noticed it was down and then helped themselves to the guinea pigs. Fencing contractors up and down the land must thank their lucky stars upon the advent of a storm. I had reached an age where I knew my own limitations in life and it was fair to say that putting up a fence that would last more than one week was beyond me. Selling was my main forte, convincing people they wanted to buy something they actually didn't realise they needed. I had learnt to speak Corporate over the years, it was what made the business world tick and if you spoke the language you could use it to sort out a variety of situations both inside and outside the work environment.

This was reinforced by an abundance of training courses down the years that had helped shape me into the well rounded individual I had become. I likened myself to some sort of Mr Corporate and this I hoped was another facet of my persona that made me invaluable to the company.

Mad Dog had been very quiet since the phone call and we decided it was best to leave him alone, much like that dreaded wasp nest that lurked in the garden shed. Grateful for the peace we kept ourselves busy motoring through our workload until an emailed invitation appeared out of the blue from Human Resources. This mysterious invitation bore the title 'Update Meeting' and was to be held at four o'clock that day. There was nothing to suggest what this meeting was about and we shot each other puzzled looks across the desks.

'Boss, what's this HR meeting all about, there's no agenda?' asked Terry, one of the newer recruits.

'Oh, they are coming down from Head Office to update us on some changes' he responded from the other side of his screen. It occurred to me at that moment that he was avoiding eye contact for some strange reason. Whenever anyone senior came down from Head Office it sparked the usual conspiracy theories that they were going to announce our office would be closed down and the work swallowed up by our northern head office. In a bizarre way it was what spurred us on to over-achieve every year and therefore make it impossible for them to wield the axe. Okay, so the business had suffered thanks to the recession but it was the same for everyone. We simply had to keep speaking the corporate speak and walking the corporate walk, the rest would follow. That's what Mad Dog drummed into us and that was the message I'd conveyed to those around me. I saw the recession as a small challenge, survival of the fittest and we were bionic marathon winners carrying rucksacks laden with concrete in that respect. After all, people made their own luck in this life, I firmly believed that. Today's meeting was no doubt just another announcement about a slight restructure designed to make it look as though the company were doing something pro-active in the current economic climate.

According to the computer it was four minutes to four o'clock, although the phone display had decided it was one minute to four. It seemed there was an unwritten rule that every company should have a three minute discrepancy between the phone and computer times. I had tried to break this curse on several occasions and thought I had succeeded by asking Rob in IT to amend the phone times. For a few days the two were locked in glorious harmony until the phone decided enough was enough and surged ahead by the standard three minutes. It amazed me how much something relatively minor would eat away at you in the background, as it was gradually escalated by your sub-conscious until one day it became all-consuming and you finally accepted that something really must be done. My other issue with the time difference was that for some reason people looked at the fastest clock to determine whether you were late for work. Why? I even did it myself, as the temp rolled in at one minute past nine and I found myself staring at the phone clock and rolling my eyes across the desk at Terry who in turn looked at his phone and would shake his head. I imagined the same thing happened in every workplace.

Terry seemed fixated with the window. As it was usually impossible to tear him away from his computer screen I guessed this phenomenon heralded the arrival of our HR department. Sure enough, I could see what at first glance appeared to be a long black hearse-like vehicle drawing up. Two important looking ladies climbed out of it, clutching various files and a large briefcase. We watched as they strode purposefully towards the entrance, tearing up the asphalt drive and leaving flames in their wake as they prepared to bore us with a selection of pointless missives. The minutes between their arrival and Mad Dog getting the call seemed like centuries. For some reason the atmosphere in the office was tangibly charged with electricity. Eventually the phone rang and Mad Dog stood up, the constipated look had returned.

'Right lets go. We're in the Goldfish Bowl, bring your crucifixes and plenty of garlic' he joked, although I sensed it to be a loaded comment. We marched along the corridor towards the Bowl where the HR ladies lay in wait, I wondered what they had in store for us. At that moment I noticed Terry had clearly stopped using his anti-dandruff shampoo again, as I found myself lost in the midst of a veritable snowstorm. It's fair to say personal hygiene wasn't one of his priorities in life. I will never forget the time our office air-conditioning stopped and we all had to suffer as the malodorous little man had sat there melting across the desk. We had collectively racked our brains to think of a polite way of approaching the subject without causing him offence or undue humiliation but no such phrase or clever words were forthcoming. In the end we had no option other than to inform Mad Dog. He had listened intently to our concerns and then told us to leave it with him whilst affording us a wink. To give it an analogy, we had effectively entrusted a homicidal madman with an AK-47 and hoped he wouldn't shoot anyone. This fear came to pass when Mad Dog had gotten up from his desk at a random moment, wandered over to the unwashed one and leaned in before delivering the killer line "Terry you fucking stink". We all collectively cringed and tried to keep straight faces so that it appeared not to be a commonly held view. He had a way with words and you had to admit he got results, regardless of the casualties left in his wake.

The four of us approached the Goldfish Bowl and inside I could see the two HR ladies sat there, waiting for us to arrive. We filed in and it dawned on me that I had made the cardinal mistake of being the last person in the room, which in real terms meant there weren't enough chairs to go round. So the next few minutes were spent trawling the building for a spare. In the end I borrowed Mary's chair from Accounts, she must have popped outside for a cigarette but I was banking on her not having the temerity to interrupt our important meeting to reclaim it, if she even realised it was there. Upon re-entering the room I sat down and noticed they had a presentation ready on the plasma screen bearing the title 'Restructure for Success'. Ironically this could have been useful advice for the uglier of the two, who would've benefited from some plastic surgery. She was in her early fifties and had clearly had a hard life. This was not helped by the fact she was short, rotund and sported a sour face that carried many wrinkles from years of frowning. The second lady was taller and in her thirties, with strangely vacant eyes and I suspected a similar personality to boot.

'Thank you for attending at such short notice gentlemen' said the first lady. As if we had any choice. I glanced around the table and everyone had the 'cut the small talk and get to the chase' look as curiosity was beginning to take its toll.

'As you are aware we are always looking to ensure we work effectively and manage our costs to maximise profitability' she continued. Just what we needed, a speech derived entirely from management buzz words that sounded important when strung together but ultimately meant nothing.

'Due to the current economic climate we have been reviewing our strategic plans for the next five years. The graph on the screen shows the projected cost of maintaining the current setup and if you look at the blue line it gives you an indication of the declining profit margins'. I didn't like the sound of where this was leading. Terry and Barry shot each other worried glances. At that moment I noticed Mary walking past the Goldfish Bowl looking around furtively, presumably for her chair.

'So we need to ensure we buy at better prices to increase our margins?' Barry interjected hopefully.

'That's right, if we can re-negotiate the procurement contracts then we put the profitability back into the deals' I chipped in. It seemed the obvious way forward, after all our suppliers wouldn't want to lose our business.

'I'm afraid all the suppliers have had to increase their prices due to the recession, we have no leverage to drive the prices down, we've tried everything' said Mad Dog with a surprisingly downbeat tone to his voice. We all stared at him in horror as the penny started to drop that something was going down here.

'So we will need to increase our costs to cover the new expenses then?' I offered.

'Not so Tim. Our rivals have reduced their prices, which will leave us in an uncompetitive position in the market.' This was another negative statement from Mad Dog who had lost all of his bark. Perhaps he should be known simply as Dog from that moment on. Out of the corner of my eye I could see Mary talking to Dave from IT and waving her hands in the air in such a way as to suggest she had no idea where something could be. I should have known she would make a song and dance about it, rather than go and find another chair. She had been at the company for many years and had become one of those dreadful employees that their manager couldn't cope with yet were too scared to take any action against for fear of reprisal. If she was on my team I would have her in shape or shipped out in no time. She was a fearsome lady and it was well documented that she had once discovered the underwear of her husband's mistress in his car. In order to make the discovery known to him she carefully inserted the garment into his sandwiches for the next day.

At that moment the younger HR lady suddenly sneezed with the ferocity of a nuclear explosion and Barry knocked his coffee all over the table in fright. This sudden reprise lifted the atmosphere and we took great delight in making groaning noises at Barry over his latest act of clumsiness. He was a bit of a buffoon at times if the truth be told.

'Will you excuse me for one moment' he uttered as he left the bowl to fetch something to clear up the spillage.

'There it is!' came an accusation from the corridor. I looked up and Mary was pointing and striding towards the

Bowl. She burst into the room oblivious to the fact we were clearly in a meeting. Rob was standing in the corridor behind motioning to me that I was for the chop and grinning away at the thought.

'Sorry Mary I heard you had been having problems with it and thought I would test it out for you' I suggested in my usual cheeky tone. I could usually get round her by deploying this tactic.

She just looked at me and uttered the word 'Prick', then grabbed the chair and wheeled it out of the room. The rest of the room were staring at me. Thankfully Barry's chair had now become available so I quickly commandeered it before he returned. Mad Dog and Terry chuckled at the thought of Barry returning to discover his chair gone. Sure enough he appeared a moment later and began clearing up the spilt coffee.

'Oh very funny guys' he blurted when he went to sit down and thankfully noticed the chair wasn't there, thus avoiding crashing to the floor.

'Go and get another chair Barry' said Mad Dog, who was becoming agitated.

'I'm fine, I'll just stand' replied Barry. And so he did, which added to the awkwardness of the meeting.

'Gentlemen, if I may continue – are there any questions on what we've already discussed?'

We had plenty, but it was becoming apparent that nothing was going to detract from what had already been decided and committed to print on the presentation. The older woman paused for a few seconds as if listening to an imaginary drum roll before commencing the mouse click that would take us to the final slide. The next page appeared on the screen with the title 'Staff Restructure' and before anyone could say anything we had all clocked the message loud and clear – there would be redundancies!

'There will be new job roles created that you are all invited to apply for, as you can see we are only holding two roles open in sales at this office and that will be to look after the existing client base' she purred. We did the maths - one of us would be leaving. I felt sorry for Barry and Terry as it was obviously going to be one of them, after all they hadn't been at the company as long as me and didn't know the Paradox system very well. Until recently Terry genuinely believed that Ebola was someone who played for Chelsea – surely that level of intelligence would be surplus to requirements. Whichever way you looked at it, this could spell disaster for one of us and whoever remained would have the guilt of knowing they'd kept their job at the expense of someone else. All of us were mortgaged to the hilt and had a certain lifestyle to maintain. This was the worst possible news and for a moment the whole event had a surreal feel to it. Nobody knew what to say or how to react. There was just total stunned silence as we sat there staring blankly like so many goldfish in a bowl.

The Day of Reckoning

Driving home after work I'd found myself imagining how Terry or Barry would feel about being relinquished of their roles. They would of course both realise that I'd be safe and therefore it was a straight fight between the two of them. It wouldn't be pretty. No doubt I'd have to go through the whole process just to make it look like a fair selection policy. We'd been informed they intended scoring us by means of a competency based interview, assessment of our past performance and also taking into account our absence record. Based on these factors I couldn't see any potential problems and besides, Mad Dog knew who he wanted. I was certain he would ensure the right people were retained by exerting his influence on the necessary area of the business even if the scores didn't necessarily stack up. The last person he would want to lose was his valued long serving employee who in his own words had a "job for life".

The red light conspiracy had taken a leave of absence for once and the traffic was moving at a sensible pace. I sparked up a cigarette and switched on the radio. Often when you needed your spirits lifting the radio somehow sensed this and provided an appropriate tonic. What would today's inspiration be I wondered?

'Statistics released today have shown a significant rise in unemployment as the recession continues to bite' came the news bulletin on the radio. Great timing, typical and topical at the same time I mused. Those figures were about to become even worse thanks to the higher echelons of management at my place of work. I guessed in a healthy economic climate many companies could afford to keep staff even if the performance was a bit below par but staring a global financial crisis in the face was a bridge too far. It felt like we were a small fishing boat being swept along in the midst of a tsunami, who knew where we would all end up? There would be others losing their jobs within the company as they made their merciless cuts. I gave the radio one final chance for redemption and switched to another station to hear the chorus "it's the end of the world as we know it". I vowed never to listen to the radio again.

Turning into the drive I saw Richard Long's red van parked outside. Despite there being enough space he had decided to park half of his red beast on our lawn, crushing a flower bed in the process. It was the little things like that that annoyed me in life. The futility of raising this sort of thing with a tradesman frustrated me - they just tended to look at you as if you were speaking complete nonsense. At the end of the day he had put us ahead of his other customers so it would've been churlish to quibble over a few geraniums. The house was its usual self as I entered the hallway. Rachel was in the kitchen preparing another of her rare yet strange concoctions that she passed as dinner. I noticed Irene was sat in the middle of the floor in a strange position.

'Are you okay down there Irene?' I asked. Presumably the sofa had finally become too comfortable, unless of course she has had one of her 'accidents' again. I was still fuming about the day she christened our brand new sofa - it had only been delivered a few hours beforehand. Every now and then when it became warm I was sure I could detect a slight residual aroma.

'If you must know I am trying to get in shape by practising yoghurt' she replied. I just despaired sometimes. Then to my horror she suddenly broke wind and it reverberated along the floor boards, amplifying the noise. There was an awkward moment where we'd both looked at each other, unsure of what to say or do next. Worryingly, I wasn't even sure if she was aware it had happened.

'Could you ask Bernard to feed the cat as I have to stay in this position for three minutes' she ventured.

'Bernard and the cat have both passed away Irene, are you having one of your moments again?' I offered her an escape route. Even if she was pretending to have a senile moment it was the easiest way to gloss over her little indiscretion. I was convinced that she used the condition to her advantage at times if the truth be known.

'Are you sure?' she replied.

'Unless those are somebody else's ashes over there, then yes I'm afraid so'.

'Oh that's a shame, I loved that cat you know' she muttered whilst staring distantly into space.

Realising this was going nowhere I decided to leave it there and inspect Richard Long's handiwork in the garden. I could see him through the conservatory window crouched down next to an alarming amount of new panels and fence posts, furiously scraping away like a deranged badger. The garden had been landscaped and cost almost as much as the house itself, but the end product was very impressive. I admired our well kept flower beds and array of perfectly positioned heathers as I ambled out into the sun drenched garden towards the hunched figure of Richard Long. The guinea pigs were making strange noises from their hutch, no doubt trying to create yet more of their species. Sadly it hadn't yet dawned on them that they were both male, but they seemed to enjoy trying all the same.

'Didn't realise the wind had taken so many panels down' I said.

'Just the six Tim, only takes one weak post and the lot comes down with it' he replied. Given that he had historically charged £100 per panel I could feel next month's commission dissolving before my eyes. How did Mother Nature know that I had a good month's salary on the way? Had she seen it coming and taken the decision to prise it from me before I'd even had a chance to spend it on something more spiritually rewarding? Such as a nice new television for the front room, or that holiday I was being pressed into booking. It was a moment of uncharacteristic pessimism for me as I could normally find the positives in a situation, an attitude which had served me well in my career to date. Positivity bred success and that in turn produced more positivity and so the cycle continued. Tim Fellows was a positive atom in a field of negative ions.

'Reckon you're all done' he stated as he hauled his large frame up from the perfect green grass.

'I feel like I have been' I replied with a sarcasm that went straight over his head.

'I'm afraid I've had to put my prices up a bit Tim, you know what with the recession and that'.

'The recession has a lot to answer for' was all I could muster in response as I visualised the final vestiges of my commission slipping away from my outstretched hand.

'What's the damage Richard?'

'It's going to be north of £700 I'm afraid my old mate' he said. Not as afraid as I was. 'I'll drop an invoice through your door'.

'No worries, thanks for coming out and fixing it at such short notice' I said. In reality I was actually thinking 'thanks for taking my commission'. I wasn't sure if this trait was specifically English, but we tended to say the opposite of what we were really thinking.

'Always a pleasure' he responded. This only served to confirm the theory. With that he swept up his tools and proceeded to head for the conservatory. As he sauntered off in the direction of the house I realised he was about to further destroy the front garden by pulling his customary wheel spin on our flower bed, but I really couldn't face trying to avert such a disaster.

That night I found it difficult to sleep and when I did finally manage to nod off I was plagued by the strangest dreams. The most recent one started off with me going for the competency based interview at work. It all started off okay until I noticed I was wearing a peculiar set of pyjama's the likes of which I would never consider owning. They were white cotton with blue cross work pattern all over and even sported a fetching breast pocket. Luckily for me the interviewer hadn't even noticed. Brilliant! He asked me to explain why I wanted the job, to which I started giving my reasons and it then became apparent as I spoke that the interviewer had paws instead of hands.

'Is something wrong?' he asked me. Was this part of the test? Would I fail if I mentioned the paws? I decided not to say anything, just in case.

'Carry on, I'm ready for the question Noel' I said.

The phone rang and the interviewer appeared to be speaking to someone, periodically nodding in agreement. After a short while he put the phone down and looked solemnly at me.

'He says you've played a good game and he likes your positive nature. So the offer is this: Take the 50% pay cut and relocate to Edinburgh or leave the company with £7,000'. I did the maths and this seemed a terrible deal. I looked around for inspiration but the walls had been replaced with the inside of a red and white striped circus tent. I looked back at the interviewer but he had been replaced by a large dog that was now growling aggressively. I felt sure this was one of those dangerous breeds of dog that the media were trying to outlaw.

'You're nothing to me anymore' it uttered with complete contempt, before leaping over the desk and proceeding to attack me in a violent frenzy of unprecedented rage. When the attack was over I lay there staring at the night sky in my blood soaked cotton pyjamas and wondered whether to just play dead or make a run for it. At that moment the moon was eclipsed by the silhouette of a macabre clown, who stood over me grinning inanely. I woke up in a sweat and decided to abandon all attempts to sleep. Clown dreams were never desirable at the best of times. I reassured myself that I had nothing to worry about and accepted it had simply been a bizarre dream, probably inspired by the feelings of guilt I felt about keeping my job over the others.

The days leading up to the competency based interview passed quickly, before I knew it the hour of judgement had arrived. I felt confident that everything would be fine and pondered how to offer my condolences to Terry or Barry when it became apparent one of them would be getting the bullet. I sat in our expansive kitchen and munched on a bowl of oats whilst reminding myself of the positive examples I would be describing to the interviewer that would demonstrate my usefulness to the company. The television was once again on, with nobody actually in attendance. I really struggled to understand the mindset of someone who purposefully turned on an electrical item and then just left the room. An advert caught my eye for a documentary about people from different demographics that had been made redundant. It was thoughtfully entitled 'On the Scrapheap'. As a nation we seemed to exhibit a curious obsession with anything that went remotely wrong until it had been morphed into a total catastrophe. Then we'd spend forever dissecting it to death before finding a new molehill from which we could create a large mountain. I considered myself lucky not to have such things to worry about, but even from my ivory tower I still saw the effect it had on the people around me and I didn't take any pleasure from it. I looked out into the garden and the shiny new fence panel s glistened in the morning dew, reminding me that Richard needed paying. Nonetheless it looked to be a pleasant day outside and this enhanced my optimism that the day's outcome would match the early promise offered by the weather.

The journey to work had been strangely pleasant, which was a godsend as I was feeling particularly jaded from a poor night's sleep. Even the red lights were kind to me, if you ignored the fact I jumped one in order to keep the positive experience going. As I entered the building the receptionist was sat there texting on her phone, barely making any attempt to hide it. I could've been anyone.

'Do you know what time those beasts from Human Resources are coming down today?' I asked in an attempt to get the information before my colleagues.

'Can I just stop you there' she requested whilst raising her hand in an authoritative manner. The art of conversation lived on.

'That's better' she muttered and then to my indignation she continued typing away on her mobile phone.

'Are you able to check, as a favour for your most favourite colleague of all time?' I requested cheekily, trying not to rise to her dissuasive manner.

'Why doesn't Barry ask me himself?' was the sarcastic reply I received as she got her phone out again, no doubt to read the response from the person she had just texted a moment ago. It was no use, if she knew and wanted to tell me it would've happened by now. Rob the IT technician was sat in reception, reading the paper and swigging a latte.

'Sorry to hear you're leaving' he said with a stony expression.

'I heard they are getting rid of the people with crap job titles first' I responded. How we laughed when the email came round congratulating him on his promotion to Senior Helpdesk Incident Technician. He had never been allowed to forget that acronym and for added irony he was largely regarded as being hopeless at fixing computers. We usually ended up solving the problem ourselves and then retrospectively told him what we'd done to fix it. Anything that couldn't be fixed by re-booting had to be logged and would then ultimately enter into a large black hole and never see the light of day again.

'They usually go for the big earners, get them off the payroll' he responded, after all his professional pride had just been wounded. Seemed a bit harsh, but then I had asked for it. You lived by the sword if you were going to engage in such banter.

'You should be safe then' was all I could think of by way of an equally cutting remark. He huffed and buried his face in the paper again.

We hardly spoke all morning, the three of us bound by the tension swirling around us like an invisible force, gradually tightening until we were virtually mummified by it. Terry was sweating profusely and I observed that he really shouldn't have worn a blue shirt on a day like this. We did have a fan in the office but we'd only use it if someone had left paperwork all over their desk and made the foolish mistake of walking away for a few seconds. We would then take great delight in switching on the fan as the victim made their way back to the desk. The look of abject horror as they saw their paperwork ascend into the air from a distance and began to run back to their desk was priceless. It was childish humour but these little pranks helped to pass the time of day and conversely it all served to enhance the sense of belonging we felt. I tried to envisage how the dynamic of the team would be affected by the loss of either Terry or Barry - things would never be the same again as each had their own traits that made the office what it was.

Eventually the time was upon me for the interview. Terry and Barry had been for theirs already and I told myself they were saving the best for last. Especially as in their eyes it was just a formality, so that they could tick their boxes and cover their oversized behinds in case of any dispute further down the line. As I approached the goldfish bowl I could see a short bald man in his late thirties and an older woman who was poised with a note pad. Upon entering the room the shiny-headed interviewer stood up and it was apparent he was virtually the same height standing as he was sitting. I hoped he wasn't one of those angry little men that had been psychologically scarred by his diminutive height and used this to vindicate his decision to ruin other people's lives as a result.

'Hi you must be Tim. I'm Ian Hepworth-Jones, head of Marketing and PR. I'll be facilitating the interview today and Susan here will be making a few notes. I've been chosen to carry out the interviews in the interests of impartiality in case you were wondering'. He made it sound so much more important by using the word 'facilitating'. I'm not even sure that word suited the scenario, but now was not the time for splitting hairs. I recognised his name from the directory however he was fairly new to the business and based at the head office. I would have preferred someone that already knew me but nonetheless remained confident.

'Good to meet you Ian' I gushed in my best Corporate voice.

'As you are aware we will be taking various factors into consideration, such as your performance and attendance record over the last twelve months, together with your score from this interview.'

'Sorry, I thought for a minute you said last *twelve* months?' I gasped.

'Yes that's correct, did HR not cover this?'

'They didn't specify the time frame I just assumed they would look a bit further back than twelve months!' I said in a slightly higher pitch than normal. This was seriously bad news, as I sat there it dawned on me that my order bank had diminished over the last few months and I had taken a few more sick days than in previous years. All were genuine illnesses, at least they sounded convincing when I'd described them whilst hanging my head upside down off the side of the bed. I recommended this tactic to anyone who cared to listen. If they looked back a few years they would see a rising order bank as I strode from success to success like an Olympian athlete at the top of his game. They would even see a period of three years without any sick days whatsoever. Okay so that was before I perfected the bed trick, but not many people could show such a clean record. No, it would all be fine I kept telling myself -the cream would rise to the top as the saying went.

'Shall we start?'

'Ready when you are Ian'. It seemed a bit familiar calling him by his first name but it was too late.

'Okay, can you tell me about a time in which you failed to deliver?' was the first question. That was a tricky one, I tended to forget such things and concentrate on the positives. Finally I came up with something.

'There was a situation whereby I agreed a supply price with one of our biggest clients Tompkins International and it then transpired we couldn't meet the order due to an unexpected shift in the market'.

'What did you do to resolve it?' he asked impassively.

'Well, we managed to reduce our margins and meet them halfway with the promise of a bigger reduction on future business once the market had picked up'. I replied with a wave of renewed optimism about the interview.

'Was this strategy your idea?'

'Certainly was!' I responded confidently.

'How many units have they ordered since, bearing in mind I can check the sales records to verify this?' he asked smugly. I wanted to climb across the desk and wipe that smile off his rotund little face.

'Erm, that particular firm switched to sole supply with one of our rivals' I admitted. There was no point lying, in hindsight I realised it was a terrible example to have given and I shouldn't have revealed the customer's name. On to the next question which would hopefully be kinder to me.

'Moving on, can you tell me about a time you made a decision that proved to be the wrong one?' For fucks sake, where was he getting these questions from? What sort of interview was this? I was starting to feel quite apprehensive and hoped that maybe it was just the first few questions that were like this. I glanced down and could see he had four sheets of paper littered with questions and I was already struggling at question two! The clock on the wall ticked loudly in the deafening silence as I tried to think of a good answer. The ticking was becoming like a drum beat, I was surrounded by voodoo people who were baying for blood and Ian Hepworth-Jones was the Witch Doctor, preparing to inject me with the poison of his choice.

As each question rolled out from his conceited lips, I felt myself becoming increasingly frustrated at the fact every question had a negative slant that rendered my carefully prepared positive examples useless. I really wanted to convey a sense of how good I was at my job and get the passion across that had allowed me to convert opportunities into success down the years, time and time again. Instead I found myself giving barely relevant answers to the hideous questions and then tried to twist them to suit the scenario.

Finally we got to the end by which time I felt like a zebra attempting to make its way across the African savanna with two hungry lions hanging from its back. I just hoped that Barry and Terry had found it just as hard and provided even worse answers than mine.

'Can you tell me why we should consider employing you for this role instead of your counterparts?' he asked. At last a reprieve - a question I could actually answer.

'I can demonstrate the best order bank year on year, I know how to get the best out of our clients and I fully understand our marketplace and their needs within it. I am rarely ill and have developed my understanding of the Paradox system to such an extent they have replaced the manual with two words – 'Ask Tim'. Seriously though, I do have an excellent knowledge of the system and use it to help troubleshoot around the business and reduce the likelihood of expensive errors. I am able to communicate at all levels and excel at building productive business relationships. In summary I am a capable performer able to work under pressure and to deadlines, employing a less capable person would result in a higher error rate and less business ultimately costing the company money in the long run'. I felt a cathartic sense of relief as everything I had been trying to convey came tumbling out in one verbal volley that I had aimed right between his ears.

'Thank you Tim, unless you have any further questions?' he offered as a wrap up, showing no emotion whatsoever.

'When will I be informed of the results?' I asked.

'Your interview score will be fed back to HR and they will hold a meeting with you all later today. It's only fair that we let everyone know as soon as possible'. Reading between the lines the rough translation was that they wanted to get somebody off of the payroll as soon as possible.

I stood up and shook Ian with the silly name by the hand and left the bowl, wondering if I had done enough to justify keeping my job. It would have been preferable to have shaken him by the neck in all honesty. I really wasn't expecting to find myself feeling so apprehensive after the interview and for the first time the reality of losing my job seemed an actual possibility.

When I got back to my desk, Barry was at lunch and Terry was pre-occupied with emptying the contents of his drawers and consigning various files to the bin.

'I'm guessing the interview didn't go too well for you?'

'I've been meaning to do this for ages' he lied.

'Did Barry say how he got on?'

'He said it was just a typical competency based interview - that was all he said'.

'Typical? I have never known such negative questions in an interview!' I retorted.

'Tim, you haven't had an interview for over a decade, the world's moved on mate, they're all doing this sort of thing now'.

'The world has gone completely mad Terence'.

The evening arrived and with all the day's excitement I had forgotten we were going out for a meal. Rachel had booked us a table at our favourite restaurant in town although I really couldn't have been less in the mood for such an event. Still, maybe it would prove to be a welcome distraction. As we drove into town, against the throng of the rush hour stragglers Rachel continued to obsess about the holiday. I was content to sit and stare at the array of onrushing vehicles as they lurched towards us and then drifted off into the obscurity behind. I wondered what was happening in their lives and what the evening held for them. My brain was frazzled after the interview from hell and was barely functioning. Even so, it was in better shape than the driver of the adjacent car, who was pre-occupied with emptying the contents of his nose. An email had been sent inviting us to the final meeting tomorrow that would involve feedback and the decision we had all been dreading.

'We won't be able to take as much as last year' she stated.

'No' I replied distantly.

'And I hope the air conditioning works this year I'm not going through all that again'

I had stopped listening to be honest. Years of practice had taught me to listen to just the last few words and then formulate a response that sounded like it fitted the conversation. She had mentioned air conditioning and the overall tone of her voice was one of discontent.

'No not again' I mumbled.

'Did I tell you Leona got the sack from Beadles?' Oh Christ what was that? I hadn't been listening at all.

'Fiona got a sack full of beagles?' I enquired hopefully. She looked at me as if I had started taking recreational drugs.

'Beadles - she got sacked Tim. I don't know what she'll do now, there's no work around. I wouldn't want to be looking for work what with the recession and everything.'

'Well, you make your own luck in life. Good things happen to good people and all that' was the best response I could muster. I didn't really want to allude to any fears of redundancy as I knew it would only serve to cast doubt over the holiday and instead create more unwanted pressure. Not only that but I didn't want to admit to myself that it was a possibility as the prospect of losing everything we had built was inconceivable. In the back of my mind I was fighting visions of being told to leave the company and tried to counter it by thinking of Mad Dog saying I had a job for life. That was always a reassuring statement to fall back on, like a mantra. It served to cocoon me in an invisible shield that was in-penetrable, deflecting all negativity away effortlessly.

'There's no such thing as a job for life these days' she remarked. In my mind I now saw myself sat dejectedly amidst the tatters of my career.

The Day of Reckoning had arrived. It was overcast outside, a lone magpie sat in the plum tree in our garden. It was a good job I wasn't one for superstition, although if the starling was anything to go by it could be time for a change of philosophy. Irene was sat in the front room eating a banana with the skin on and the television was on yet again. She wasn't even watching it therefore I assumed it must be for the benefit of the dust mites. Naturally everyone would complain when it finally stopped working after the cumulative wasted hours of its life had taken their toll. The clock seemed to be moving faster than usual today, I wondered why time passed so quickly when something you were dreading was looming. I just needed to keep positive even if the worst should happen I would find another job so it was a win-win situation. Yes that was right, Tim Fellows would survive this and pluck victory from the jaws of defeat! I didn't know why I was even panicking, on paper I was worth far more to the company than Terry or Barry and anyone in their right mind would work that out and make the right decision. It was just that something about the interview had spooked me.

I arrived at work to find Barry and Terry embroiled in a typical debate. 'What's the moral dilemma of the day then boys?' I asked.

'Would you rather have no hands or no feet?' Barry replied. We often indulged in this game in the morning.

'Easy, no hands' said Terry, looking pleased with himself.

'Why's that Terry?' I was fascinated to hear his rationale for this.

'I could still play football' he exclaimed.

'That sounds plausible however there is one small flaw in your plan – you play in goal' I shot him down in flames. It was a sport that we enjoyed. It was so typical of Terry, he never looked at the bigger picture.

'Have you ever been to Amsterdam?' asked Barry.

'No, are you thinking of going?' I answered.

'It's on the bucket list'

'Oh, what's on your bucket list then?' enquired Terry.

'Just Amsterdam' Barry replied nonchalantly.

'Morning men' barked Mad Dog as he entered the room, looking somewhat dishevelled.

'Heavy night was it boss?' asked Terry.

'Yes she was, that's the last time I try internet dating. She said the medication had affected her weight since her profile picture was taken. I think it's more likely her propensity towards fast food if the truth be told.'

The three of us looked at each other and shuffled back to our desks to embark on the day's work. For a brief moment it was as if everything was normal, the banter amongst the band of brothers was in full effect and a casual observer wouldn't realise that the axe was about to fall on one of us.

We tried our best to work efficiently but the truth was that everyone was on edge, as the morning wore on our nerves became increasingly frayed. Eventually Terry made a strange yelping noise akin to a puppy in pain, which signified the arrival of the beasts from HR. We shot worried looks at each other. We hadn't really discussed how we felt about the whole situation as nobody wanted to acknowledge how it would affect the team. Men don't tend to discuss such things in my experience.

After an eternity Mad Dog's phone rang, shattering the tense silence.

'Okay, I'll send them round' he said soberly, before putting the phone down and letting out a dejected sigh.

'Alright boys, can you make your way round to the Goldfish Bowl and wait outside. They will call you in one by one. I wish you the best of luck' he stated. Why did he look at me when said that, maybe I was being paranoid. The three of us scooped up various items, more out of nervousness than the fact we actually needed any of them. For example, Barry was holding a small rubber hedgehog, which we bought for him as an in-joke many moons ago. I took a pad of paper and some screen-wipes. This was not a time for rational thought. We trudged around to the Bowl in virtual silence as colleagues gazed at us as if we were diseased, with red crosses painted on our foreheads. They were obviously aware of the fate to be bestowed upon us in the next few minutes and felt the need to add to the morbidity. There were two chairs that had been placed outside the Bowl - of course there were only two. So we each quickened our step to try and get there first without actually running. The problem was solved by Terry, who stumbled over his own feet with just a few yards to go. Barry and I quickly seized the opportunity and grabbed the chairs. Maybe the fact there were only two chairs was meant to be symbolic, or maybe it was just the fact there were never enough chairs in the building. I suspected the latter.

We sat there in silence, with Terry stood over us like an awkward spare part. It occurred to me the chairs could've been the final test to determine which of us would go, whoever was left standing being deemed the weakest link. I decided against sharing this thought, as Terry was nervously playing with his hands and Barry was chewing his rubber hedgehog. I took out a screen wipe and started cleaning the metal parts of the chair arm supports. The silence was deafening as we waited and after it became intolerable I decided to say something to break the tension.

'The vending machine in the toilet is full of condoms but the headache pills have sold out. That tells me that most guys here are stressed and nobody is having sex' I quipped.

'That machine took my change at lunch' he replied.

'Oh, you're feeling lucky tonight?'

'No my head is banging' he explained.

'My point entirely'

One of the vampires suddenly appeared at the door of the Bowl and beckoned for Terry to go in. He sauntered in and shot us both a rabbit-in-the-headlights look as the door closed behind him. As much as I liked him I found myself hoping that when it came down to the wire, they would ask him to leave and not me. Selfish I knew. It seemed astonishing that our whole careers were about to be defined in the moments that lay ahead.

'Can you hear anything?' I asked Barry as he was sat nearer the door.

'Nothing Tim' he replied after glancing in with absolutely no attempt to mask what he was doing. Terry had his back to the door. After some time and lots of nodding from both Terry and the vampires, he stood up and came towards the door. We both sat there looking expectantly at him, for some sign of how it had gone. He just looked at us in the same rabbit-like way and said 'You're next Tim' before slouching off down the corridor. I hoped that not being first or last meant I was going to be safe, either they had just told Terry the bad news or were instead saving it for Barry, who sat haplessly next to me.

'Hopefully see you on the other side' I said to Barry as I stood up.

'Roger Roger' he replied. I was equally unsure of what he meant by that, but it sounded like bad news for Roger. My heart was beating like a giant festival bass speaker and the cone was threatening to break out through the wire mesh as I entered the arena, the two seated beasts hungry for the kill.

'Sit down Tim' ordered the older one. I can't imagine

what else they thought I was going to do.

'Thank you for coming, as you know we are here today to discuss the results of the competency based interview and let you know the overall outcome with regards to your application'. For some reason the use of the word application made me feel like an outsider, despite nearly two decades of service.

'We have had feedback from Ian Hepworth-Jones about the competency based interview and he said that you were a likeable and enthusiastic man and gave a good interview overall'. I made an internal sigh of relief at this assessment, he has clearly seen through my half-baked attempts at answers.

'He did say however, that he felt some of the answers you gave were not entirely relevant to the questions and that you could have given a bit more detail in certain areas.' That was a hammer blow. I wanted to get off of the rollercoaster right now and ask to go on the teacup ride instead.

'He has therefore scored you twelve out of a possible fifteen' she explained in her monotone voice. It could've been worse —I hoped it was a better score than the others had managed.

'In addition we have assessed your performance over the last year against your target and given a score of ten out of fifteen, this is because your order bank has diminished.' This felt like an unnerving further blow for Team Fellows.

'Can you not look at the last ten years and take an average?' I said in exasperation. 'I have exceeded targets for years prior to the last twelve months. It just seems really unfair that you are only looking at the period since the recession started!'

'It's the same for all three of you I'm afraid, Tim, it's all relative' she replied. The other lady just sat there staring impassively.

'Finally we have assessed your attendance and reduced your score by a point for every separate period of absence.'

'Sorry, did you say *separate* period?' I said without trying

44

to withhold the fact I was surprised.

'Yes that's right' she replied sternly.

'But surely if someone has had a month off sick it's worse than taking two separate days off?' I quizzed the irksome woman.

'Not using the Bradstreet Factor, this method is very popular in modern businesses.' She retorted.

'Given your four separate incidents you have scored eleven out of fifteen. Therefore your overall score is thirty three out of a possible forty five.' I really didn't know what this meant in real terms without knowing the other scores.

'So where does that leave me?' I asked, sinking into my chair.

'Your score compared to the others was very similar in all areas except the absences, which I'm afraid has reduced your overall score to less than Barry and Terry's' she delivered the killer line without a hint of sympathy or remorse. In that instant everything I had worked for had been discarded like yesterday's news. I was consumed with anger, despair and anxiety all at once as I tried to come to terms with the bullshit this woman was spouting at me. My head was spinning and I felt short of breath, everything I had built up had just crumbled and been shot down in flames by the fucking Bradstreet factor, whatever that was. How could this have happened? Years of exemplary service and performing to the best of my ability had been undone by a few sick days and a ridiculously flawed interview with an idiot from another office who knew nothing of me. I had to get out, get some air - get away from this suffocating room and the poisonous creatures within it. I stood up and made for the door.

'Please Tim, do not divulge anything to Barry' she said as I was leaving, that was the least of my worries. I stumbled past Barry and strode towards the exit, desperate for some air to refill my constricted lungs. I could see faces staring, the same faces I had worked with for years but now strangely distant and cold. The world spun like it had never spun before and I stumbled out of the building, along the drive and into the busy street. As I stood there looking up at the array of towering buildings it struck me that I had never felt so small in all my life.

The Urban Jungle

And so it was, nineteen glorious years had been brought to a swift conclusion by people that barely knew me. In the days following my 'release' from the company I had found myself contemplating what I could've said or done differently - each time produced a different conclusion. No matter though, the outcome remained the same. I sat by the study window and watched the smoke drifting aimlessly from a suburban bonfire as it slowly dispersed into the early evening atmosphere - in many ways mirroring my career. Much like the burning detritus beneath the flames I had served my purpose and been found to be surplus to requirements, extinguished and thrown out without a second thought. I considered myself a survivor and would of course find another employer -you couldn't keep a good person down as I always said. But in the meantime I felt entitled to mull things over and try to make sense of everything, if that was at all possible.

It struck me that far more sinister motives had been at work, perhaps there was a grain of truth in Rob's rebuke that they always laid the higher earners off first. If that was the case, they would've tailored the criteria to whatever was needed to influence the final outcome. Therefore nothing on this earth could have prevented the inevitable. In some ways that thought made me feel slightly happier about the situation, although conversely also served to increase the associated sense of bitterness. I didn't usually buy into conspiracy theories although they were fascinating sometimes - but something just didn't add up. Terry and

Barry were both nice guys but with all due respect I knew in my heart of hearts they were inferior. Yet for some reason they were still sat at their desks while I resided on Castaway Island pondering my next move.

In the days leading up to the competency based interview and various meetings I had let insecurity creep in but held onto the 'job for life' statement that offered so much re-assurance in my darkest hour. Some comfort that phrase was now. It made me realise that people meant what they said at that moment in time, but the harsh reality was that things changed in life and such words soon became distant echoes.

The final few days had passed quickly. I'd spent them tying up loose ends and having the 'pleasure' of handing over my nineteen years of hard work to the people that had kept their jobs over mine. It had come to light that Mad Dog's own position was under review, no wonder he didn't want to rock the boat by insisting I was retained with my inordinate salary. I had been a veritable sitting duck in reality. It wasn't a case of just poking my head above the parapet - I had unwittingly danced around no-man's land whilst holding aloft a flashing neon sign that displayed the words 'high earner' at the onrushing enemy forces. It was beyond torture having to train the others in all honesty. I did it with dignity but it felt like a final twist of the knife, as if actually making me redundant hadn't been enough of a body blow. Colleagues would come over and say things like 'remember it's the job that has been made redundant not the person' and I knew they meant well but they couldn't see the flawed logic in that very statement. I wanted to respond by saying 'that's great I will be in Monday then' and observe their subsequent embarrassment as they tried to back track. I knew deep down they weren't deliberately being insensitive and were purely trying to say something, however useless, rather than say nothing. Which incidentally was the approach taken by some, who behaved as if I'd contracted the plague and would avoid eye contact, or any contact for that matter, at all costs. Not the treatment you would expect after years of working in the same space, where you believed bonds had been formed that would survive the test of time.

My final day had been surprisingly bearable - I just wanted to get out of the place and on with my life by that point. There was the expected card and ritualistic humiliation of opening presents and having to give a speech in front of everyone. As was customary they also wanted me to provide cakes which I thought was a bit odd considering I would need every penny going forward. Surely they should be buying me cakes? Mad Dog had thanked me for all my hard work and the general consensus was that I would be greatly missed. I toyed with the idea of mentioning the 'job for life' comment in my speech. Ultimately I thought it best to appear gracious, in case one day they asked me back when it all went tits up. I had scooped up my desktop possessions, photo frames, Paradox certificates and 'Salesperson of the Year' awards and left to a chorus of well wishes for the future. Rachel had picked me up from outside, as they apparently needed my company car back immediately. I looked back at the building as we drove away and noticed they had all gone back inside before we'd even climbed into her VW Polo, charming. I had felt a strange mixture of excitement at the adventure that lay ahead, mixed with a certain amount of trepidation at the same time. When people had told me about various traumatic events in their lives I had historically struggled to empathise without having the necessary similar experience to draw upon myself. I had to hope that some things would never be inflicted upon me. So there it was: jobless, bereft of a car, no private health cover, sick pay, bonuses or structure within which I could serve a meaningful purpose. All in all, the situation I now found myself in represented a worrying state of affairs. I was however confident that with my track record, knowledge of Paradox and overall persona I would be able to secure another job and we would be able to maintain our current lifestyle. The alternative didn't bear thinking about.

As I sat there and reminisced by the window my thoughts were rudely interrupted by the piercing noise of the smoke alarm sounding downstairs. I rushed downstairs into the kitchen expecting to see a large fire engulfing the room and instead Irene was stood there wearing nothing but a scarf. She was busy pushing marshmallows into the toaster.

'Do you want yours toasted Tim?' she said as she turned round, revealing parts previously untouched by man.

'No thanks Irene and I think you should get some clothes on. You really shouldn't be using the toaster you know'.

'It reminds me of sitting round the camp fire in the Scouts'

'Irene, you weren't in the Scouts! Now please get some clothes on' I was losing patience.

'Okay okay I'll wait for mine, could you bring them out Timothy'. Did she really just call me Timothy? Was this how it was going to be from now on - me sat at home having to constantly baby-sit Rachel's insane mother? If I needed an incentive to find another job, this was surely it. She handed me the pack of remaining marshmallows and wandered out of the kitchen, hopefully she would be getting dressed. I turned the toaster off at the wall and started scraping the burnt marshmallow from the metal filaments. The early evening was upon us and the throng of workers across the town were no doubt making their way home from another busy day's work. I realised how I had taken that feeling for granted for a long time. Suddenly the doorbell sounded, I abandoned the toaster and made for the door. Before getting near it I could see a stranger through the opaque glass, stood there expectantly in the soft glow offered by the evening sun. I toyed with the idea of ignoring him but the problem was, he had already clocked me. I opened the door to an older man wearing a suit and pinned to his breast pocket was a rosette, which signaled his allegiance to a political party of some description.

'Hi, I'm Brian Furbishley, your local MP. You will be aware of the local elections and I wanted to go through our manifesto if you have a moment or two?'

'Er, that should be fine' I replied, but the truth was it really wasn't fine. Once again I found myself saying the opposite of what I actually meant. I had rarely actually entertained a doorstep caller and found myself unsure of the protocol in this situation. Are you supposed to invite them in or do they expect to stand there? I decided he could stay outside - he needed to know his place.

'That's great, the first thing we want to do is help the local youth gain employment with various initiatives that we have devised.'

'Have you got any plans for the local adults that are out of work?' I asked.

'Do you mind me asking if you are out of work?'

'I do mind, but yes I have just been made redundant' I replied a bit too abruptly.

'Oh I see, I'm sorry to hear that. The thing is, most adults have already gained work experience and therefore have a skill to offer employers whereas the youths are finding it hard to convince people to give them a chance'.

'Surely you should be focusing on the adults who have mortgages to pay and responsibilities, ultimately we are looking after these youths that you describe'. I felt a tasty debate coming along and wondered why I had avoided this sort of thing in the past..

'That's a fair point but the youths hold the key to the future of this country and we have to nurture them in order to build a successful infrastructure. That's not to say we're neglecting the older demographics, they are just as important'.

'Do you have any schemes or plans for the 'older demographics' then?' I had to ask the question.

'Not currently but do you have any ideas? We're always happy to listen to your suggestions' he countered, placing the onus on me to come up with the solutions.

'Moving on, we are actively involved in promoting awareness of the elderly in our constituency who may be vulnerable during the winter and in need of extra help with heating and........insulation.'

I wondered why he paused and then noticed he was looking over my shoulder. Turning round I already knew what to expect and there it was, Irene stood there in all her naked glory holding an umbrella and eating a marshmallow.

'Do you want me to freeze to death?' she asked nonchalantly before strutting off towards the kitchen. I turned round to face the MP and tried to think of any plausible explanation for what he'd just witnessed. Instead we just stood and looked at each other. I could see in his eyes he was puzzled and he could no doubt tell from mine that I had no answer. The silence was interrupted by the shrill sound of the smoke alarm in the kitchen again.

'Sorry, got to go' I said and shut the door in Brian's face. As I made for the kitchen I glanced back and could see Brian's silhouette as he was stood in the doorway still. These MP's never knew when to give up. As usual they were busy alienating themselves from the real people by concentrating their efforts in the wrong areas. But then what did I know? I wondered if he realised that most constituents simply turned up at the polling station and voted for the name they liked the most. The very same voters then scratched their heads and wondered where it had all gone wrong months down the line. I strongly believed the majority had no idea of the policies their chosen parties were planning to adopt. It never ceased to amaze me that polling stations had nothing displayed that clearly set out each party's policy. At least the uneducated could then read the facts and make an informed decision before casting their vote. If democracy worked in the country's favour it was more by luck than judgement.

The evening had descended upon us and we sat watching the daily soaps after dinner, Irene was standing in front of the dining room mirror holding the remote control.

'What is she doing now?' I asked Rachel as quietly as I could.

'I heard that!' retorted Irene averting her gaze from the mirror.

'Just leave her Tim, at least she's quiet' scowled Rachel.

'Okay but don't start moaning at me when she turns the channel over at a crucial moment'

'I thought you hated the soaps anyway'. It was true, I hated them with a passion but they served to remind me that whatever sort of day I've had there was always someone worse off.

'Richard Long called earlier' she announced.

'Oh right, what did he say?' I asked despite having no actual interest in the answer.

'Just said he'll catch up with you later, after his money no doubt' she replied. I made a mental note to sort out his payment, although in truth it wasn't the greatest priority.

'So how was the job hunting today -have you managed to find anything yet?'

'I've been busy scouring the internet for something suitable - I'm going to head into town tomorrow and see what the agencies have. With my experience it should be a walk in the park.' That was partly a lie however I truly believed good things happened to good people. In a world where people changed their jobs more often than their underwear I hoped future suitors would be impressed with my lengthy commitment to one company.

'That's funny Tim, you spent all day staring out of the window' chirped Irene from behind me. Rachel shot me a look that would turn most mortals to stone.

'Thank you Irene' I responded, whilst motioning to Rachel that Irene was barking mad. She seemed to buy it - I really need to get out of the house during the day before Irene caused any further trouble. At that moment the television channel changed. I gave Rachel the 'I told you so' look and she retaliated with the 'fuck off Tim' expression in return.

'I can't get any other channel on this wretched thing' said Irene as she walked away from the mirror.

'Horror channel was it Irene?' I asked cheekily, Rachel kicked me in the shin. I was quite pleased with that quip until I happened to glance around and catch Irene sticking her middle finger up at me. This whilst pulling the increasingly familiar 'fuck off Tim' face.

I had awoken with much optimism for the day ahead. Today was going to be the day that Tim Fellows went out to the big city, let the business world know of his availability and then had to choose the best position from the array of offers that would surely follow! I could see it now and could almost feel it......almost. It was surely going to be a formality –in a short space of time I could visualise myself negotiating perks such as a company car, fuel card and other associated delights. After spending the previous day of feeling sorry for myself I had found a renewed vigour and sense of determination. Much like a Neanderthal hunter venturing out from his cave in search of a meal for his family I would return triumphant to a rapturous applause.

Clutching my file, which contained CV's and certificates, I left the house just after eight in the morning and headed towards the bus stop. There was a crisp chill to the morning air and I could see my breath as it hit the waiting atmosphere and then dispelled. I realised as I approached that I hadn't used the bus service for over a decade. In fact I hadn't used public transport in any form, I preferred to drive everywhere or pay for taxis. However, the distinct lack of a car had put paid to that. An assortment of characters of various shapes and sizes had already gathered at the bus stop. Not wishing to appear new to this scene I strode confidently towards the timetable and started running my index finger down it. In truth I had no idea what I was supposed to be looking at and turned round to a youth who was stood behind.

'Hi, I'm trying to get into town - do you know which

number bus I need?' I enquired. As a general rule I tried to avoid the local natives. The youth removed his ear phone and frowned.

'Ask your friend over there' he responded whilst beckoning to another guy who was stood just on the edge of my peripheral vision. I turned round and observed a scruffy man in his mid forties with his hands down the front of his trousers. He looked to be a jelly baby short of a packet. What puzzled me more was that nobody seemed to notice and if they had they weren't remotely bothered. Was this normal behaviour? Surely it couldn't be, if I carried on like that in public I would fully expect to be arrested within minutes. I decided it was best to just wait for the next bus and see what was displayed on the front as these reprobates were of no use to man or beast. Finally a bus arrived after what seemed like an eternity and I wasn't even sure what to ask for. Thankfully trousers man was not getting on the same bus. As we pulled away I watched him slide past the window and disappear into the distance. I hoped I would never see him again.

As the bus weaved its way through the less affluent parts of town the quality of the people boarding it seemed to deteriorate. At one point I felt like I was aboard one of those vehicles they used to transport criminals around the country to various courts. I looked completely out of place, like an aardvark amongst a pack of Senegalese Parrots. It struck me that the cost of the journey was actually more than the fuel it would've cost me if I had driven. Yet still the government tried to persuade us to use public transport, where you were thrown into the same space as people you would normally avoid. To compound matters you then had to endure the tinny sound that represented their excuse for music as it surged out of their earphones and frazzled the last vestiges of their brain matter in the process. I realised how protected I had become over the years from mingling with real society - cocooned within my comfortable lifestyle where I didn't have to do anything that I didn't want to. Well, except looking after Irene. I had been so sheltered by my safe existence that taking a bus into town seemed such an alien activity. It shocked me just how many shops, flats and houses had become boarded up and were slowly rotting into complete dereliction, victims of the recession's poisonous reach. I wondered who had owned them and what their stories were, tried to imagine the heartache the former occupants must have endured as their lives were undone and dismantled. The more you owned, the more you lost - that was how it was. Some of those poor people had barely owned anything of real value but they had lost it nonetheless, the end result was the same. I hadn't realised at a grass roots level how much the recession had affected us, that was until now. It was hard to visualise the prospect of our house being re-possessed and all of us being thrown onto the street, for which I would feel entirely responsible. The thought of this eventuality made my heart uncharacteristically race and I decided not to dwell on it.

After what seemed like an eternity the bus arrived at the train station and I wandered into the main entrance and climbed the never-ending flight of stairs in search of the ticket office. Walking around the ticket Kiosk it became apparent that it was un-manned, and had been that way for some time. Jesus, even the station had become derelict. A piece of faded paper had been stuck on the inside of the kiosk window that simply said 'Use Ticket Machine'. So, with this helpful advice in mind I trekked back down to the machine and finally worked out which ticket to buy. Could they not have put a sign at the bottom of the stairs highlighting the fact it was pointless going up them to buy a ticket? I chose my ticket and put a crisp ten pound note into the required slot. The machine whirred and flashed lights, then spat it back out. I tried every possible permutation and each time it returned the note. And they said this was progress, there was no substitute for interacting with an actual human being. A voice from behind interrupted the cash rejection process.

'Allow me Sir-I had the same problem just the other day.' A skinny man presented himself. He looked respectable enough and seemed to know what he was talking about. I had to put my trust in someone. That was until he took the note and ran off with it. Is this what the world had come to? I pressed the 'call for assistance' button and a buzzing noise was followed by an automated message stating that nobody was available to help. Again I wondered why anyone would put themselves through the experience of travelling by public transport. Eventually after what seemed like another eternity I finally managed to convince the machine to take a note and made the ascent to the station. The platform was relatively busy and it was just starting to rain. I stood under the cover of the dilapidated roof and took in the aroma of cigarette butts and urine that seemed to permeate the fabric of the place.

Suddenly a man appeared from out of nowhere and stood uninvited in my personal space.

'Have you got a ticket?' he rasped, looking me dead in the eyes. I started searching my pockets for the ticket.

'Yes thanks' I replied, wondering where this was going as I remembered where the ticket was.

'I'm with the Transport Police, can you show me some ID' he demanded. I went to reach for my wallet and at that moment noticed the smell of stale alcohol on his breath. Furthermore, he didn't even look remotely like an official of any description. I realised I was being hustled again.

'What's the matter? You know it's an offence to refuse a police officer' he was starting to take on a more aggressive tact now as he stepped up the hustle. My mind was racing as I tried to work out the best way of managing the situation. No amount of corporate jargon was going to see off this desperate man who appeared to have nothing to lose. I was aware of people watching but none of them were compelled to intervene, instead they preferred to keep out of it. I wondered what I would do if I was them. At that moment the train pulled in and the distraction was enough for me to slip past him and blend in with the swarm. In my rush to get onto the train I walked straight into a large African woman that was trying to get off, losing my balance in the process. I quickly scooped up my folder and leapt on the train before the hustler spotted me again. As the doors shut I could see him cornering a fresh victim and it dawned on me as the train pulled away that this was just part of being in town for most people.

After fifteen minutes of being crushed and enduring a bearded man's breath that had the aroma of a decomposing wildebeest, the train eventually rolled in to the heart of the city. At one point he was so close I suspected he was trying to start a family with me. I had seen people refer to 'commuter hell' on Facebook and today I able to relate to it. So this was it - the day Tim Fellows would show the world that he was a capable and employable example of the human race, defying the recession propaganda. Just as soon as he had found some coffee and maybe a cheeky salmon and cream cheese bagel.

Sitting in one of the many cosmopolitan coffee shops that had sprung up I found myself deep in thought about the events of the last few weeks. In many ways it was an exciting prospect having to start again at a new company, where I would be an unknown quantity and likewise they would be to me. I wondered if I would ever have left if my hand hadn't been forced. Although there had been pressure at times it really was a relatively easy existence in hindsight. I sat and stared out of the window as what seemed like hundreds of people buzzed past, like busy ants scurrying about their business. They appeared to be headed in aimless directions in a singular sense, yet all for the greater good collectively. I wanted to be a part of that again, instead of an unemployed and unpaid carer. Out of the corner of my eye I realised someone was heading towards me. Even worse than that, judging by his demeanour he appeared to be a vagrant with that distinctly dishevelled look and generic limp that befitted such unfortunate people.

'Excuse me good sir' he uttered in a surprisingly well-spoken tone.

'Morning' I replied and then swiftly resumed staring out of the window in the hope he would then move on to the next person. He didn't.

'Is anyone using this chair?'

'Er, no that's fine you can have it'

'Thank you squire, you're a gentleman and a scholar'

Thinking that was all I breathed a sigh of relief. Then to my absolute horror he just sat down in the chair next to me. I glanced furiously around the cafe and there were more empty tables and chairs than occupied ones. I could not believe what was going on. Even worse was the aroma that emanated from this transient which presumably was a fusion of stale smoke and alcohol. I stared in disbelief as he rifled through the pockets of his grey trench coat whilst muttering incomprehensible words to himself. Then, out came the obligatory rolling tobacco pouch and he began to roll, with hands that looked like they had been run over several years ago by a tractor and then set on fire.

'If you think they're bad you should see my feet' he admitted. I hadn't realised how obvious my staring had become.

'Yes I think I'll pass on that thank you....' I replied.

'They all stare, they all judge' he countered.

'They do a lot of things' was all I could think to say.

'I was like you not so long ago' he rambled. I doubted that claim somehow.

'Take my advice son...'

I waited for this earth shattering advice. The waiting continued as he constructed his rolled cigarette.

'And your advice is?' I eventually gave in. Not only had he invaded my space but I now had to drag information from him that I didn't even want to hear. It was becoming increasingly harder to hide my revulsion at his malodorous presence.

'The buck always stops with the man at the top of the tree. Don't be that man. There's more to life, I've lost everything but never been happier'. There it was - the revelation of the century. For some reason every tramp claimed to have been a success prior to their downfall.

'If I don't find another job I may be joining you' I tried to empathise with him.

'Be careful what you wish for son, how you define success is what ends up defining you' he muttered, running his withered hands through locks of matted grey hair. Clearly this man of the streets was the last person I should be taking advice from.

'Well I will bear that in mind' I replied as I made to leave. At least he hadn't asked for money.

'I don't suppose-'

'No I haven't sorry' I replied cutting him short before leaving the coffee shop and its resident prophet of doom. I must have one of those faces that people from all walks of life feel they can just start talking to me.

As I breezed along the bustling high street I saw the first recruitment agency sign jutting out in the distance and prepared to make my grand entrance. I strolled confidently past the array of derelict shops and small family owned stores and observed forlorn shopkeepers looking hopefully at the outside world. It was the same look on every face I saw. The sun decided to make an appearance and suddenly the world seemed a much better place, for some reason this gave me a renewed sense of optimism. As I reached the door to the agency I raised my hand to the glass and pushed hard in order to make a positive entrance, before almost rebounding off of it. The door was locked to my complete surprise. I looked down and saw a small mountain of post piled up on the other side and then it struck me that the interior was in fact bereft of people, computers or furniture. Not the best start, I hoped they had been involved in the wrong market sector and that this wasn't a sign of things to come.

Undeterred I continued along the high street, past an array of beggars and yet more abandoned shops. The world was walking in the opposite direction of course and I had to keep sidestepping people who regarded me as invisible and were hell-bent on walking straight through me. After the third such incident I decided to try the game out for myself. I decided to simply walk in a straight line and let the world step aside for Tim Fellows for once. Seeing a gap I set my trajectory and strode purposefully forward, God forbid anyone who got in my way. The first couple of opponents seemed to take notice of my determined stride and moved out of the way, it was all about displaying confidence I told myself. I had learnt this from many a corporate course. The third opponent also stepped aside, this was becoming too easy, it struck me that such positivity was needed to steamroller my way towards a new job. This optimism was about to face its toughest test as it became clear the first few victories were mere ripples in the ocean. I was now faced with a tidal wave of pedestrians heading towards me and this new sea of people looked in-penetrable. I carried on regardless and as we headed towards each other I got a sense that a game of chicken was being played out. Who would hold their nerve the longest, me or the onrushing tsunami? I decided to hold my nerve and locked eyes with the person directly in my path as we both locked onto each other's co-ordinates. I kept my determined stare and he tried to return a similar look but I sensed as I was nearly upon him that he was starting to waver. Time seemed to have slipped into a slow motion mode as we prepared for impact, this one was going to the wire and I felt like a single Spartan going into battle against an army of bloodthirsty Persians. The moment of impact was upon us, collision was unavoidable unless one of us moved. Suddenly his face changed with a millisecond to go and he ducked out of my purposeful stride and I took a second to shoot him a victorious glare as I passed. Sadly in my moment of triumph I hadn't noticed the lady in the electric scooter behind him and it was too late by the time I did. Falling over the front wheel I tried to keep hold of my folder but had to choose between keeping my face or the leather bound collection of CV's. The face won. I managed to break my fall and ended making some sort of commando roll before ending up on my back as pages of my CV landed around me. I could see silhouettes of the relentless pedestrians as they stepped around me, looking down with faces that knew they should help but conceded they were far too busy. The milk of human kindness had run dry. As I sat up the elderly lady in the scooter stared at me with a face clearly ravaged by the hardships bestowed upon her urban life.

'I'm terribly sorry, are you okay?' I asked, despite being the one who had come off worse. I was conscious that people were walking all over my CV's around me but felt obliged to wait for her answer. It failed to materialise, instead she shook her head and rode off into the sun. I picked up a page of my CV and felt yet more despair at the symbolic footprints all over it. The town seemed to be walking all over me, just like my previous employer. Scooping up the rest of my CV's, I put them in the nearby bin, keeping just a few saveable copies. As I glanced at the row of shops to my left I realised this whole sorry event had happened outside a recruitment agency. A lady in the window had obviously been watching and quickly scurried away when she had been rumbled. The problem was I couldn't pass up any opportunity so I braced myself and walked into the agency, with my confidence dragging along the floor behind me.

As I entered the agency there were three desks occupied by women, with no indication as to who dealt with which employment area. So I headed for the first desk and took a seat opposite the twenty something brunette. I became aware of sniggering to my right and caught sight of the other two pointing and laughing before hurriedly trying to appear as if they were actually busy. The girl in the window had obviously seen everything and couldn't resist pointing me out to her colleague. At that moment I realised I had never felt so stupid in my working life, or been exposed to the jungle that was the urban high street. A life of milling around in taxis and company cars from one executive suburban meeting to another had shielded me from the realities of the world. We ate in the same safe restaurants, drank at the same public house and did most of our shopping out of town or on the internet. Our holidays had been to exotic locations. The day had only just begun and already I felt like an impala in the lion enclosure at the local zoo.

'Can I help you sir?' asked the brunette politely. I was guessing she was unaware of my fall from grace outside in the street.

'Yes, my name is Tim Fellows and I have just been made redundant. I'm looking for a new role in executive sales or something similar, I don't mind something a bit lower with scope to work my way up' I ventured.

'Have you registered with us online?' she replied.

'Er, no I prefer to do things face to face, it all seems very remote online'.

'Oh, it's just we ask people to register online, where you can upload your CV and fill out the questionnaire. We then send you some aptitude tests to complete for the latest software packages. It's just so that we can gauge your ability as some of our clients are quite particular.'

'Is that really necessary? I've been in the same job for years and have extensive knowledge and experience of the Paradox system'. There, I had played my trump card.

'The what system?' she asked to my complete surprise.

'Paradox, you must have heard of it. Lots of the bigger companies use it' I replied with an assured tone of voice.

'Mr Pellow, I'm afraid I've never heard of it, perhaps it's one of those bespoke in-house packages rather than the more commercially available programs' she countered. I felt like I was shrinking into the fabric of the chair.

'Its Mr Fellows' was all I could muster, as I contemplated

the fact that the Oracle system and associated knowledge of it may not be so desirable to future employers.

'Sorry, I'm terrible with names. Here's my card, if you go to this website and follow the registration prompts we can then get you set up and email the tests. Do you have a CV with you?'

'Right, so I have to register online first?' I questioned.

'Yes, I'm afraid we are very busy'. I glanced around and the agency was empty.

'Do you have many vacancies in executive sales?' I enquired hopefully.

'We do get them although at the moment a lot of employers are moving towards telesales as they try to save money, what with the recession and everything'.

'Okay I will register online then I guess' I replied with a semi-sarcastic tone of voice. I reached into my folder and retrieved a CV then passed it to her. She looked at it for about one second and placed it onto a pile of other people's CV's. I had visions of them just shredding the pile at the end of the day.

'Thank you for your help' I uttered as I got up from the chair. I decided to deliver the sentence in such a way as to make the recipient wonder if I was being sincere or sarcastic. In truth, I was shocked how ridiculous the whole conversation had been. She had seemed more obstructive than helpful, I felt sure this wasn't normal and reassured myself that the next agency would be more sensible. It was however a surprise to learn that Paradox was not widely used. Had I invested my time and energy learning the intricacies of a defunct program? I may as well have told her I was an expert in the Courgette system.

Once again I stepped onto the high street and took on the sea of onrushing pedestrians and inbred mutations although this time opted out of any attempt to walk straight through them. I just hoped that agency was the exception rather than the norm, or else I would be the next homeless man dishing out advice in coffee shops before long.

Fellowship in the Ring

The rest of the day continued in much the same vein as the morning, as I trawled the various agencies it became apparent that nobody was remotely interested in actually finding me a new role. This was mostly down to the fact there seemed to be a glaring dearth of vacancies. The few hand-scrawled jobs described in the window were nothing more than a hook to entice the unsuspecting masses through the door , once inside their CV's would be exchanged for false hope and the victims sent on their way to repeat the process elsewhere. I hadn't realised just how depressing an experience this was going to be. Of course I had my Paradox knowledge and years of sales success but the reality was dawning on me that the streets were littered with hordes of Tim Fellows who were all beating the same path as me, walking slowly in the wrong direction on a fast moving conveyor belt to nowhere. How long before we were all unwittingly swept into the abyss I wondered. At that moment as I sat in the market square watching the world go by I noticed my optimism seemed to have deserted me. Was this the harsh reality of being on the scrapheap? Before this I had known exactly who I was and where I was going. I felt like a big fish in a small pond. I had my place and I liked the certainty it provided. Now it felt like I had lost my identity and the worst part was that people who had been a large part of my life had suddenly gone. Their absence left me alone with a deafening silence and just a few distant echoes. The sun seemed to have taken the afternoon off and it was unusually dark for three o'clock in the afternoon. Storm clouds seemed to be gathering in more ways than one. I started to wonder what might happen in the long run should work not be forthcoming. There were financial pressures that came with running an expensive house and we were highly geared in that respect. This was one fact that I knew existed but tried to avoid thinking about, the preferred approach was to bury my head in the sand. The thought of filling my days looking after Irene filled me with abject horror too. I imagined pursuing a new hobby such as golf or potholing just to keep out of her way. Still, this was only the first day of trying to find work and at least I had my redundancy money to fall back on in the short term, a minor comfort. I had heard of people being made redundant and their employer had failed to pay anything, resulting in lengthy battles and no short term solution for the income deficit these poor people faced. I guessed there was something to be grateful for at least. As I sat and indulged in some covert people watching I happened to notice the job centre across the square and wondered if it was worth a visit, even if just to rule it out as a viable option. In my situation I couldn't afford to be too selective. If we wanted to maintain the lifestyle to which we had become accustomed I was going to need to pull an industrial sized rabbit out of the hat. The last time I had experienced a job centre was in the halcyon days of my youth, when everything was quite simple and I had my whole working career ahead of me. Up until recently I was very pleased with how life had turned out, the trophy wife, daughter, a respectable house in a nice area, expensive holidays and a valued employee at work. I still had the majority of those things, but the vehicle that funded them had broken down and while my back was turned somebody had towed it away. I needed to get that vehicle back on the road or face the prospect of everything slipping away. Keep it together Tim I told myself.

As I approached the job centre I wondered if it had changed since my last visit all those years ago, even back then it seemed archaic and stuck in a time warp. I recalled looking at various boards with the jobs they claimed to have available written on postcards that had been shoehorned into slots. You would then have to decipher the handwriting to decide if the job was suitable and after finally convincing yourself it was acceptable to earn such a paltry amount of money you would then traipse over to the endless queue and wait expectantly to be seen by a woman with more facial hair than yourself. She would look you up and down like something that had crawled out of a dog waste bin and then call the company to try and convince them you were the right candidate for the job. Then only to pull a face that resembled a mistreated mule and inform you the vacancy had been filled some time ago and they had neglected to update the boards. I remember thinking I would never get that wasted time back. The worst part as I recalled was having to rub shoulders with the dregs of society who seemed to inhabit such places, finding ever more inventive ways to extract 'emergency payments' to solve an unexpected crisis. Reading between the lines this amounted to a lack of alcohol to numb the pain of their wearisome existences for a few more hours. Who were they fooling? Apart from the hapless pen-pushers behind the teak veneer desks who seemed determined to dish out the taxpayer's money to those reprobates without too much by the way of qualification. I had even witnessed some of them head straight into the nearest pub minutes after cashing their 'emergency payment' at the post office.

I wandered through the double doors and instantly the familiar aroma hit me. Yes, it was the smell of the unemployed layabout characterised by stale smoke and a general lack of personal hygiene. I recognised it immediately, it never leaves you. Some things never changed. I glanced around furtively, half expecting to see the handwritten cards

67

on boards. It appeared the new protocol was to stand in a queue and explain to a gatekeeper the nature of your enquiry and this person would then decide where you should go and point you in the right direction. Clearly the unemployed couldn't be trusted to choose one of two directions that were clearly signposted upon their arrival - to the extent they need someone to herd them like sheep into the correct pen.

'Good afternoon sir can I help you?' enquired an overly friendly employee who clearly wanted more out of life. His teeth glistened like a collection of large glaciers in the sun.

'I'm just looking thanks, I was made redundant and need to find a sales role' I replied.

'Oh I'm sorry to hear that, I was made redundant once it's a terrible experience, I know exactly how you feel'. He seemed to think we were now best friends.

'Well it's far from ideal but I expect to be able to find something else fairly quickly'. He looked at me as if I had just made the most ludicrous statement since the dawn of time.

'It's tough out there at the moment. I am seeing good people like you coming through these doors every day. There are far less jobs than people out there'

As much as I was enjoying being told the obvious it wasn't really helping my quest to find work.

'Have you tried the agencies on the high street?'

'I have been into most of them yes but they just referred me the internet'

'We have a very comprehensive website with all of the latest vacancies. If you register with us you can receive all of the alerts for your chosen sector. If you log on to **www.governme-**'

'Is there somebody here that I can speak to?' I interjected before he could finish.

'Yes of course Sir, you can speak to me'

'I meant to sit down with someone and register, go through potential vacancies etcetera'

'Do you have an appointment?'

'Well no, I was just passing and-'

'You need to register first, then we will give you a date to come in and be interviewed, it's usually about two or three weeks if that helps'. It didn't really.

'How do I register?'

'Through the website Sir'

'Of course you do' I replied without concealing my growing contempt. Was it no longer possible to do anything without involving the internet? At that moment I found myself wondering why I had bothered to dress smartly and brave the Public Transport system just to be told to do everything on the fucking internet. There should just be a sign on the window that says 'Don't bother coming in, it's all on the website'. I wondered what the world was coming to as I turned and shuffled dejectedly out of the building, towards a large imaginary drawing board and an expectant household. Like chicks in a nest they would be sat there waiting for good things to be brought to them. But today their luck would be out it seemed.

That evening we sat around the dinner table, a rare event in itself, Irene was staring wistfully into space and I found myself wishing I could do the same, absolve all responsibility and just let someone else worry about everything. There were certain subjects that for financial reasons I wanted to avoid discussing.

'I've been thinking about the holiday' said Rachel. That was one of the subjects.

'Oh....what have you been thinking?' I asked hesitantly.

'I think we should book the flights and accommodation before the prices increase further'

'Increase any more?' I tried not to sound too exasperated.

'I told you, the package has gone up by two hundred since last week'. I could see pound notes burning in my mind's eye at this point. I had no recollection of this conversation taking place. Herein lied the flaw in my practice of listening to just the last couple of words.

'Oh right, yes I suppose we should look at that'. Irene

tutted and looked up to the heavens.

'Richard Long was outside earlier, I said you would settle up with him this week for your fence'. Apparently I had taken sole ownership of the fence since it collapsed.

'There was some post for you earlier' she uttered as she passed me a small handful of envelopes. I could already see they were mainly credit card bills and junk mail. The credit cards in particular were a cause for concern as the redundancy money was only just enough to pay the bill off. But I needed that money to pay the mortgage and sustain our lifestyle until a new job had been found. I felt a momentary flutter of panic at the thought of our predicament, in particular the problem we would face if the credit cards called in their debts unexpectedly. Surely that couldn't happen I hoped, but then who knew what was in the small print? Rather than 'Terms and Conditions' these booklets should have been named 'Our Get-out Clauses '. I had heard of some unscrupulous lenders getting into a panic due to the recession and trying to protect themselves by calling in their debts and virtually bankrupting people in the process. It was all wrong in my opinion but to these companies it was just business and in this climate they could argue it was dog eat dog. As consumers we were all dogs.

'So Tim, did you have any luck with the agencies today?'

'Well, not exactly' I replied, really not wanting to discuss it.

'Not exactly? What does that mean in real terms?' she sounded annoyed already.

'Oh, everywhere I went they just told me to log onto this and email that, nobody actually sits down with you and tries to help any more. They just refer you to the bloody internet'. Irene shook her head and put it in her hands, her face looked solemn as it made its way down to her waiting wrinkly hands. At that moment I wondered exactly why I was bothering to try and appease these two ingrates.

'You'll need to have found something by the holiday!' barked Rachel in an almost hysterical fashion.

'It will be fine honey' I rebuked.

Great, so no pressure then. I wanted to tell her to get a fucking job instead of swanning around having her nails done and sipping expensive coffee with her irritating friends at my expense. I wanted to, but I didn't. There was nothing to be gained from it, apart from a few days silence while she sulked like a petulant child. Her sulks were legendary in that respect. At that moment it dawned on me that I had subconsciously been avoiding conflict on any level over the recent years by letting her have her own way, the old adage of 'anything for a quiet life'. The small flaw in this plan I feared was about to become apparent. In fact that small flaw had the potential to become a cataclysmic and cavernous rift if the dreaded word 'no' started creeping into our lives. Just at that moment, rightly or wrongly I felt a bit aggrieved at the house of cards that I visualised as being precariously perched before me. In my minds eye there was a rusty old weathervane just behind the house of cards that was starting to rotate in expectation of an onrushing tornado. I imagined the consequences of everything we had built being torn apart and scattered as we desperately clung on to anything that could be salvaged, least of all our dignity. I felt a slight twinge in my chest at the thought of that and hoped it was only a worst case scenario. I longed for those days when I used to sit and stare out of the window and wish something new and exciting would put me to the test, take me out of my comfort zone. I would give anything to either go back to those ignorant days, or at least travel back in time and shake some sense into my younger self. Maybe I could have said or done something differently that would have prevented the redundancy.

Amongst the letters I noticed a brown envelope with no obvious origin. Intrigued I opened it with the dinner knife, much to Irene's dismay, and saw the letter was from my former employer. Maybe they had seen the error of their ways and retracted the redundancy, it had all been a mistake and they had meant to release Barry instead. My heart raced, could it be? The momentary excitement was quickly replaced by dismay however. It was a letter advising they had arranged for me to attend a free course that was designed to help people back into work. It was part of their redundancy package by all accounts - I must admit that during all of the turmoil I hadn't read through the paperwork in great detail. There could have been a clause that we had to adopt a Polar Bear as part of the process for all I knew.

'Look at this, they have sent me on a course' I offered to anyone who was listening.

'When are we going?' asked Irene nonchalantly.

'It's next Thursday apparently. Oh and luckily it's in town so I only have to spend a small fortune getting to the free course and then there's lunch to pay for too' I replied, sidestepping her attempt to join me.

'Did you hear that dear?' I asked Rachel, who was more interested in vacantly staring at her mobile phone. She didn't answer. If it didn't affect her, she zoned out of the conversation it seemed. If I had offered to buy her a diamond ring she would've heard that I had no doubt.

'You should go Tim, you never know – it might teach you something' replied Irene, in a rare moment of coherence.

'Maybe I should just go on an internet course instead' I responded dejectedly.

'My husband went on a course once and I haven't seen him since' she countered, clearly the moment of clarity in her muddied brain had been short-lived.

'Have you had a good day?' I asked Ellen in order to change the subject. She had sat quietly eating her dinner so far.

'Don't change the subject Tim' Irene answered on her behalf.

'I didn't realise you two were the authority on job seeking, it's a fucking jungle out there!' I snapped and with that stormed off upstairs like a tantrum hurling child. The trouble was I knew they were probably right. But it was incredibly grating to be patronised by those two freeloaders, one of whom never worked and the other who couldn't recall doing so. As I trudged up the stairs I hoped this new found bitterness wasn't going to be a feature of scrap-heap Tim, I didn't like feeling scornful and miserable and now it was starting to affect how I behaved at the dinner table. What next? I had visions of sweeping everything off the table and throwing Irene through the dining room window in an uncontrollable fit of rage. The solution was simple - I just had to find a job. I poured myself a consolatory whiskey and sat on the bed, letting out a deep sigh. At that moment the familiar vibration of the phone started in my pocket, a cursory glance at the screen revealed the caller to be Richard Long. I pressed the reject button and sank the whiskey like they do on the films, except I had forgotten how strong it was in reality. Still, a bit of extra heartburn couldn't make much difference when added to the increasingly regular twinges I had experienced in the chest of late.

I reflected on what had been a humbling yet somehow interesting day, braving the onrushing throng of the town, amid the cacophony of sounds, hustlers and general discordance. For the first time since I could remember I felt uncharacteristically pessimistic and lacking in general confidence and in need of some serious divine inspiration, not least intervention. Maybe the course was the answer. I decided to give it a go, apart from the house and all of our aspirations I had nothing to lose.

In the days that followed I tried several more times to join the agencies and applied for vacancies online. All of these activities proved time consuming and ultimately bore as much fruit as a large cactus. In desperation I called the number on the crumpled letter I had been harbouring as a last resort. The clock was ticking and every wasted day was another step nearer the abyss. True to form, even the course involved an online registration - but then what else was I to expect in this cyber-pseudo age in which we existed. If it wasn't on a screen, it wasn't real as far as society was concerned in this modern age.

It was the day of the course. When I originally saw the invitation my first reaction was one of contempt, followed by a concession that there was nothing to lose. At the time I would not have thought it could be my last resort. That sounded dramatic, even for me, but the clock had been ticking and so far nothing had changed. So maybe I needed this course to change my perspective. I would never have expected a few months ago to be travelling by public transport to attend a course with a selection of rejects, with a subject matter of gaining employment. It was all so easy back then and I didn't realise it. I had all my ducks in a row back then and almost everything had been nicely in place. I felt very vulnerable now and this was amplified by the removal of benefits that I had previously thought nothing of - such as healthcare cover through my employer. If I had became ill historically I would have had the option to use my private healthcare to fix it. Ironically I didn't have any need for such cover while I had it – but now I was only too aware of its absence. With that benefit taken away from me, along with others I felt less protected and strangely humbled by the big wide world.

The course was being held in what appeared to be a decrepit former government building that had seen better days. Even just by walking in the doors of the place you could smell the eighties, engrained into the very walls and performing a recurring nod to the past. For some reason it reminded me of my first day at school, being taken to this scary place and having to meet new people in a new environment that smelled of times gone by. I recalled that despite my trepidation at the time, I soon settled in and realised that it wasn't going to be so bad after all. This despite the fact I had inadvertently broken an unusually speckled bird's egg that the teacher had brought in to show us on day one. I remembered the teacher launching an enquiry and various accusations being bandied about while I sat quiet and tried to work out what was best to do. Eventually when it seemed an innocent person was receiving the final blame I had to do the right thing and come forward with a teary confession. At that moment I was totally immersed in the memory of that long gone day, when I became aware somebody was trying to attract my attention.

'Is that you Tim? Are you here for the Employment Skills Course?'

'Caitlin? Er, yes sorry I was miles away' I replied, in a distant way as if woken from a dream. This was confusing, as I hadn't seen this lady stood before me for quite some time and seeing her out of context had thrown me. We had worked together many moons ago and had forged a good friendship, often staying late after work to chat. Sometimes it would get very late and we would lose track of time, resulting in a crazy dash home and fabrications about traffic congestion. She was someone that I had always looked out for and I felt we had a good connection. I remembered feeling sad when she left the company. We had kept in touch but over time our paths went their separate ways as often happened, even with the best of intentions.

In perfect synchronicity we both said 'It's great to see you', then both laughed and to try and break the cycle we then pointed at each other and mouthed 'Ah'. I thought this could go on forever.

'So what are you doing here? Have you joined the redundancy club too?' I asked

'I have been working abroad for the last couple of years, teaching English. Got back and apparently there are no jobs in this country anymore!' she replied.

'Wow, we must catch up properly it's been too long'

'Definitely, first we need to get through this weary course. The job centre put me down for it' she explained.

'At the moment I have more chance of flying to the moon strapped to the back of a large rock than getting a new job' I analogised whilst giving a cheeky grin. Caitlin chuckled at the quip. I had forgotten how I used to like making her laugh. It was a pleasant surprise to see her again after all this time and I found myself looking forward to the day all of a sudden.

We headed along the almost derelict corridors towards the training room. As I surveyed the surroundings I imagined this could be the set of a survival horror film, with hapless individuals dodging hordes of blood lusting un-dead inside the filthy labyrinth. It was the perfect setting for such an event. As I looked inside the various empty rooms that we passed I wondered what it had been like in its prime. How many people had come to work here day in, day out, only to be mercilessly told to pack their possessions and leave their posts when they were deemed surplus to requirements? There was no loyalty in business. I could smell Caitlin's perfume and it reminded me of distant days, happier days, it was nice to feel that familiarity again in these troubled times. Suddenly the room was upon us and I felt an unexpected trepidation at the prospect of what lied ahead. Caitlin burst into the room and it appeared they were already underway.

'Sorry we're late, is this the time management course?' I offered in an attempt to break the ice. The room was silent.

'You must be Tim and Caitlin?' said a portly lady whose attire matched the era of the building.

'Yes I'm Caitlin and this is Tim' I countered, thankfully this time to mild chuckling from the onlookers and a playful slap on the arm from Caitlin.

The chairs were set out in a circle and we took our seats on the only remaining ones available. It was reminiscent of a group therapy session.

'We've just been through the introductions, perhaps you would like to tell us all a bit about yourselves?'

'My name is Tim and I am....an alcoholic' I said, which received an outburst of laughter from the others. Suddenly I found myself showing off, the fool's version of having something interesting to say.

'Sorry, I'm Tim Fellows. I have spent most of career

working in sales for the same company. I am apparently institutionalised as a result. Oh hang on, I should be institutionalised'. More laughs ensued. I was starting to enjoy myself at this point.

'Thank you Tim. Caitlin, how did you come to be here today?'

'I came on the bus' she replied. I laughed out loud and a couple of others joined in.

'Where were you working before this?' she re-phrased the question without cracking a smile.

'I have been working abroad until recently. I'm looking forward to this workshop as it's a fucking nightmare trying to find work these days' she said, clearly unaware she had included profanity in her statement. The course instructor didn't know where to look or what to say, a few glances were exchanged around the room.

'Well, I'm Jean and I have been running these courses since the recessions in the nineties' she finally informed us.

'And still wearing the same clothes' I whispered in Caitlin's ear. She laughed a little too loudly.

'Would you like to share the joke?' rasped Jean, all eyes were on us.

'No thank you' replied Caitlin without batting an eyelid. I was taking proverbial cover at this moment.

Glancing around the room I took a moment to perform a mental run down of the other course attendees. There was a mixture of different demographics, much to my delight as I was expecting a selection of middle aged cast offs similar to me. This demonstrated to me that people from all walks of life had been affected, although I knew it was wrong to take comfort from that, I couldn't help it.

The day seemed to be passing quickly and Jean made an effort to involve everyone and make it more interactive. It was so much better that way - the best courses I had attended were of this ilk as opposed to listening to a trainer's monotonous diatribe whilst hoping for death. We learnt a variety of useful tips as the day wore on. Not least that you should try and appear several times at a prospective employer's premises for seemingly innocuous reasons before an interview. That way your face would seem familiar to them. I quite liked this idea and made a mental note to put the theory to the test. We also learnt to match the body language of the interviewer, mirroring their every move and then once synchronised you could theoretically start to dictate the movements. The idea being the interviewer would then subconsciously follow you and this somehow shifted the dominance from them to you. Again I made a note to try this, if indeed I ever managed to secure another interview. The main focus of the course was to teach you to employ a different and yet often untapped methodology. Jean told us that we should approach companies we would like to work for, as this was deemed to be far more impressive in the eyes of employers. It also yielded the highest success rate comparatively she had assured us.

The course drew to a close and we filed out of the building. It had been a much more beneficial day than I had imagined and I felt a renewed wave of optimism. Another unexpected surprise was the chance to rekindle the friendship with Caitlin. We stood outside in the glow of the late afternoon sun - the golden hues gave Caitlin's face a warm radiance as she spoke exuberantly about her time abroad. Her eyes sparkled hypnotically and I found it hard to concentrate on what she was saying as I was thinking of our late night chats from the past. It was great to have a friend like her, who was so interesting and engaging and I realised I had really missed her being in my world. We said our goodbyes and I looked forward to seeing her at the course the next day.

The bus was full of the usual assortment of characters all crammed into a small space like refugees from a war torn country, the available air seemed a little thin and I felt strangely claustrophobic. I sat and stared out of the window at the world as it passed by. Market traders were busy packing up their wares for the day and office workers raced against each other to reach the station a millisecond quicker than the next man. School children were loitering outside fast food restaurants where they had de-camped and no doubt chewed over the day's events along with considerable saturated fat. For some reason they usually felt the need to communicate with each other via the medium of shouting, desperate to be heard by the world. I recalled such days, when testosterone raged through me unabated and I wanted to be the best at everything I did. This was tempered by the gradual realisation that I wasn't setting realistic goals for myself and led to inevitable frustration. As I'd grown older I came to accept that I couldn't be the best at certain things but there was nothing wrong with trying all the same.

That night I sat and mused over the day's events after the usual torture that most people referred to as dinner. I sat in my room and caught up with some much overdue administration on my mobile phone, liking the status updates on Facebook that had been posted by people I'd either never met or hardly knew. It seemed like a poor substitute for living a meaningful life, following other individuals and living through them in effect. I searched for Caitlin and to my surprise there were thirty seven people with the same name and hardly any with pictures I could recognise as her from the few pixels my phone afforded me. Suddenly I had an unnerving sense of being watched and hurriedly tried to close the current view on the phone, managing only to drop it onto the bed with my searching activity on full show. Irene was stood there looking down imperiously whilst brandishing a clutch of envelopes courtesy of the postman.

'These came for you today' she said before dropping them on my lap as if they were caked in dirt.

'Thanks Irene, more people want paying I expect'

'A man came about your fence'

'Oh yes, *my* fence'

'I told him you don't have a fence' she said and afforded a wink. Was she actually playing up to the stereotype now I wondered?! If only it was that simple to get rid of people like Richard Long. I saw his van everywhere, the man was haunting me.

'Will that be all?' she then asked.

'Erm, yes thank you Irene, could you type up those notes for me' I said, engaging in role play for my own amusement.

'Sometimes I wonder if you're a carrot short of a fruit bowl' she replied, looking disdainfully at me. The word ironic came to mind. She turned and left, it was only afterwards I realised a carrot wasn't even a fruit.

The first area of immediate concern was the fact that most of the envelopes bore less than recent date stamps. They had been sent nearly two weeks ago, Irene had clearly been hanging onto them. The second observation was the more damning one. There was a credit card statement - apart from being nearly due the interest rate showed at a whopping 32 per cent. The minimum payment on the account was more than our monthly mortgage payment, which wasn't exactly cheap. The fixed interest period had clearly come to an end, over the years I had amassed a sizeable debt in the region of £28,000 due to a variety of different reasons. Fortunately my credit rating was astronomically good which afforded me the best rates. I simply moved the debts around onto cheaper cards and this kept the minimum payments low enough to manage. I played the system to my advantage as best I could but at the same time was only too aware it was a potential ticking time bomb. I thought it best to tackle this development quickly and made a mental note to call them tomorrow evening and perform the usual money movement. Alternatively I would invite them to offer the King of Credit their best rates in an attempt to keep the interest with them. They would be mad to turn me away after all.

Altered Perspectives

I had awoken with a spring in my step, the sun had decided to join the proceedings and I found myself really looking forward to the second day of the course. After running the gauntlet that was public transport the group had taken their seats in the Alcoholics Anonymous circle and the participants engaged in general twittering. I noticed that everyone had rushed to the same chair they had selected the day before. I thought back to the myriad of courses I'd attended historically and recalled that without fail the participants had religiously slipped back into their previous seats – it had presumably felt safe. I had been as guilty as the next person. One seat was empty today though and to my dismay that was Caitlin's. I hoped she was going to be joining us as it had been great to catch up with her yesterday. Jean looked furtively at the clock on the wall and then performed a sweep of the room before repeating the process in an obsessive compulsive fashion. She clearly didn't tolerate lateness and thinking about it I guessed it didn't fit with the whole ethos of the course. The main purpose was to ensure we were 'work fit' and ready to be unleashed on the world of employment once more.

'I'm going to have to start Ladies and Gentlemen, we have a lot to get through today' announced Jean. She seemed to be wearing a dress that looked hand made from a pair of old seventies curtains.

I looked at Caitlin's chair, she was conspicuous by her absence and the course appeared less appealing without her.

'Today we're going to be looking further at interview techniques and preparing that killer CV, the one that is tailor made to get you the job. Who has recently been to an interview?' she asked the room. There was a completely muted response as everyone looked at each other and shrugged despondently. I was absolutely shocked that nobody in the room had even secured an interview, yet once again felt strangely comforted by it.

'I've been applying for jobs on the internet solidly for six weeks and nobody has even replied' said Alastair, a burly Scottish man with excessive facial hair. People started nodding in agreement and looking around at each other for reassurance that they weren't alone.

'I've started receiving declines for jobs I haven't even applied for' I joked in attempt to lift the mood.

'Okay cast your mind back to the last interview you can remember....hang on I'm terribly sorry' Jean said, interrupted by her phone. I looked at the 'Please switch all mobile phones off' laminate on the wall and raised an eyebrow at Alastair who grinned back.

'Please excuse me' she said, leaving the room.

We sat there in silent anticipation and there were awkward moments where it felt like someone should've made conversation however small, but nobody did. I didn't really know what to say, instead preferring to gaze at my phone and look at other people's lives on Facebook. Adults were sometimes just as bad as teenagers when it came to social etiquette. I could see Jean's silhouette through the frosted glass window as she moved around gesticulating wildly in the corridor. Eventually she came back into room looking highly perturbed.

'I'm really sorry but something has come up and I need to be somewhere, I wasn't expecting *that* call today. The centre will re-book you onto the next course and refund your travel expenses if you keep your tickets' she blurted and then appeared to start sobbing before sweeping up her handbag and files.

'Hopefully see you soon and sorry again, but I must go' she said and with that, left the room in a flurry. Everyone sat there looking at each other, completely dumbfounded.

'Women eh' remarked Alastair as he hauled his portly

frame from the chair and headed for the door. Others grumbled and slowly followed suit, saying their goodbyes and looking generally forlorn at the turn of events. I sat there and wondered what I would do with this unexpected free day, maybe I could start prospecting companies that I fancied working for, make my face 'known' to them. The room was soon bereft of people so I gathered my things and my thoughts then took a slow wander out of the building. The majority of these thoughts involved Caitlin, or rather more the lack of her. I wondered if indeed our paths would cross again and I regretted not asking for her number the day before. In any event, I had more pressing matters on the agenda and decided to put these thoughts to one side while I concentrated on the priorities in hand.

I stepped out into the sun drenched city street to find it was remarkably quiet following the passing of rush hour. For reasons I couldn't explain the buildings appeared much taller than usual and it felt like they were towering over me. I had never really thought about such things before. The whole city was much more cosmopolitan these days, sporting an array of coffee shops, whole food retailers and eateries aimed at a mixture of different cultures. Maybe I would indulge myself with a Puerto Rican breakfast whilst mulling things over. My thoughts turned to Rachel, who had become increasingly distant since the redundancy. Apart from asking about the holiday and then in turn panicking that we couldn't afford it, she had shown little interest or support so far. Maybe that was a sign of her confidence that I could turn things around and get back on the employment ladder quickly. Or maybe it was a more worrying indictment of her detachment from the reality of the situation and that she just didn't care. Either way, the result was the same, I needed to find a job and quickly.

I had often wondered what would happen if a course facilitator received a call during a training session that required them to leave and now I knew. Apparently they could just abandon the course and make a run for the door. I ventured into a nearby coffee shop and upon scanning the prices it became obvious I would be spending my entire redundancy on one latte. Nonetheless, the price didn't stop me indulging in a steaming mug of their finest offering.

'Do you take cash?' I asked the rotund gentleman behind the counter.

'Er....yes we do' he replied hesitantly after computing my question. I liked to throw people off kilter a little by asking questions they would normally hear but with a slight twist. It was more for my own entertainment but if they found it funny then that was an added bonus. After a succession of whirring noises followed by something that sounded like an elephant inhaling cocaine, I finally received my latte.

'Sorry about the wait Sir' he offered - the classic lie.

'No problem at all' I replied with equal insincerity.

I wished we could just say what we really thought in some situations, the world would be simpler place. I took a seat outside at a small table overlooking the main drag of the street and reflected on the strange circumstances that placed me at this establishment. A person dressed as a giant penguin was stopping people in the street in a desperate attempt to try and sell them something. What sort of person would sink to such depths in the employment world as to undertake this job? I couldn't imagine waking up in the morning, grabbing the penguin outfit from the wardrobe and spending the day approaching complete strangers in the street. To my horror I realised the penguin had started heading in my direction. Its waddling frame lumbered towards me like a character from a child's animated film. The occupant was no doubt preparing to try and sell me life insurance or something else that didn't befit the costume at all. The penguin was advancing ever closer and I tried to hastily drink the latte but only succeeded in burning my tongue. Glancing around there was suddenly nobody in close proximity that could be spoken to apart from me. For fucks sake I just wanted to sit there and drink my latte whilst contemplating what to do next. It was too late the sun had been eclipsed by the silhouette of this black and white beast as it loomed over me.

'Good morning Sir, have you got a minute to talk about your life insurance arrangements?' came a voice from within the headpiece. I couldn't believe it was actually selling life insurance.

'I'm afraid not I'm a bit busy at the moment' I replied hoping that would be the end of it.

'You don't look very busy if you don't mind me saying'

'Excuse me?' I was astonished at the penguin's rudeness.

'You look like someone who should be on a course right now' it replied.

'Well, I was supposed to be on a course since you asked but-'

'I've heard it all before' the penguin replied holding up a hand motioning me to stop speaking.

'Look, let's cut to the chase - do I really look like the sort of person who would buy life insurance from a penguin in the street?'

'Do I look like the sort of penguin that goes around ripping off middle aged businessmen for a day job?'

'I don't even know what a dishonest penguin looks like in any event...and what do you mean middle aged?' I replied with an increasingly agitated tone.

'Well if you don't mind me saying so Tim you are no spring chicken these days' the penguin replied shaking its head, which incidentally was about to be knocked off of its sloping shoulders. I stood up to confront the irritating buffoon in penguin attire and use my height to gain back a little dominance.

'Hang on, how did you know my name?' I asked.

At that point the penguin, chuckling away to itself removed the headpiece and was none other than Caitlin. I didn't know what to say or do, but I was pleased to see her despite her best efforts to goad me.

'What the hell? Why are you doing this awful job Caitlin?' I asked without thinking.

'And your job is?' She replied with a cheeky grin.

'Fair point' I conceded, at least she had a job even if it was terrible.

'I got a call last night offering me a commission based field sales role, asked if I liked dealing with the public and was a self starter, whatever that means. I got to their office and they handed me this suit, so here I am. It wasn't quite what I had in mind' she explained, looking exasperated.

'These companies are becoming quite creative with their job descriptions in the current climate' I said knowingly. Not that I did know, but at least it sounded like I did.

'So what happened with the course?' she asked.

'The trainer blew us out after taking a call, said it was an emergency. I was just wondering what to do with the rest of the day'.

'Do you know what, screw this penguin nonsense lets go and do something cool instead' she said and began stepping out of the costume.

'What? Are you serious? You can't just throw away your promising career on a whim' I joked.

'Watch me' she replied, removing the rest of the costume and throwing it into the nearby bin. I loved her rebellious streak and wished I had some of her bravado sometimes.

'So you want to spend the day with a middle-aged man eh....'

'I was being kind' she replied sarcastically. I liked her acerbic wit - it was all part of her appeal.

'Have you ever been to an ice bar?' she asked.

'Is this a penguin reference?' I joked.

'No I'm serious, I know the guy who runs one in town. You will bloody love it Timothy'.

'Yeah why not, let's do it' I replied in a surprise moment of complete abandon.

With that we headed towards the tube station, Caitlin seemed to have an unerring ability to weave through the throng of onrushing pedestrians whereas I struggled to keep pace and dodge them with my larger frame and general lack of nimbleness.

We reached the mouth of the tube station and suddenly she stopped in her tracks and looked at me over her glasses in much the same way as a suspicious school teacher.

'Have you ever tried a penguin?' she asked.

'Are we talking about the chocolate variety?'

'No, I'm talking about the trip' she replied with a glint in her eye.

'I'm sorry, what? Do you mean a trip as in the drug?' I asked nervously.

'My flatmate gave me a tab before work this morning, I guess it was semi-prophetic, do you want to take half each? It won't do you any harm, just makes things a little more....interesting' she responded in all her vivacious splendour.

I felt like I was under some sort of hypnotic spell but at the same time the general wave of recklessness I was currently enjoying made me consider this new proposal. She produced what looked like a small square of paper about one centimetre square with a penguin picture emblazoned on it. To all intents and purposes it looked like one of those fake tattoos that children bought from dispensers at the seafront on family days out.

'Do you know what, it's fuck it Friday' I heard myself saying. It was almost like someone else was speaking for me. The next thing I knew, I had taken my first 'penguin' at the entrance to the station in full view of everyone. I wondered what had become of me but at that precise moment it didn't matter. I could feel the phone vibrating in my pocket, upon a quick inspection it was Richard Long. I rejected the call and we headed for the train.

After a short tube trip we arrived at our destination and I followed Caitlin through various unknown back streets until we reached a fairly innocuous looking building.

'Is this it?' I asked as we stood next a pair of double red doors in a side alley.

'VIP entrance' she proclaimed and then proceeded to yank them open. I was starting to feel a little strange at this point, nothing I could put my finger on specifically but I could feel my peripheral vision was starting to become a little hazy, creating a goldfish bowl effect. We entered the building and I followed her into the darkness and down a set of stairs. Before long she opened another door and suddenly we were standing in another world. Namely one that was frozen and sported an impressive bar carved from ice with various colourful neon lights refracting from its glistening form.

'Look at the lights, they're amazing' I remarked.

'They're cool aren't they' she replied, giving a nod to a bearded man in a red puffer jacket, presumably her friend on the inside. He nodded back, as if some sort of telepathic conversation had taken place. I wished I was that cool, that I could just take people to ice bars and nod at people who questioned nothing. Instead, my world had been one of corporate entertainment, sitting around with business men talking in corporate tongue about things that seemed increasingly more alien to me. We approached the bar and Caitlin ordered a jug of something called a purple turtle. The ice bar was fairly convivial with lots of different people chatting away and enjoying sharing the experience. I noted that we were the least prepared in terms of clothing, it was cold but I didn't really care. Some sort of jazz music with a fair amount of bass was kicking around in the background, giving the place an interesting atmosphere. Or maybe that was the drug I had taken. For all I knew, we could be sat in a bare room and all of this was a hallucination.

'Ironic how you threw that penguin suit away' I quipped as we sat there watching our own breath.

'I thought it made my bum look big' she said without cracking a smile. I wasn't sure how to respond. Apparently laughing wasn't the correct way, judging by the look she gave me.

'So Tim, what's the big plan now?' she asked.

'Drink Purple Tortoise and enjoy the atmosphere?'

'It's Turtle - and I meant what's the big plan for your future?'

'Ah, well I basically need to find a job that pays the same salary as my old one or start selling vital organs'.

'Is it that serious?'

'It will be if I don't find something soon in all honesty. I was hoping the course would provide some useful insight'

'What does your wife think?' she enquired.

'Rachel doesn't seem too concerned about anything apart from the fucking holiday it seems' I replied truthfully.

'That sucks, surely she must be supporting you though – is she able to take on more hours while you look for work?'

'It would be a start if she took on some hours at all. She doesn't work. We've been comfortable enough to enjoy a decent living on my money alone for years. But the mortgage has gradually grown and I have some large credit card debts too. Of course the bastards have started racking up the interest charges' I conceded.

'That doesn't sound very comfortable Tim' she replied with refreshing honesty. I knew she was right.

'On top of that, if I don't find a job I will end up spending my days looking after Irene, who doesn't know her own name'.

'So what are you going to do?'

'That is the golden question Caitlin, it seems this recession is far worse than I'd realised'.

'Something will come up. You just have to stay positive Tim'

'Yes I know, although with each day I feel like another piece of me has broken away. I miss my old job and the people – they were my friends. It's all I've known for most of my working life. Nobody knows the Paradox system like me'

'The what system?'

'Don't worry -I wouldn't expect anyone from the real world to know what it is'. I replied despondently.

'So how about you? What's your big plan?'

'I have a few options. Sorry let me rephrase that - I have few options' she joked.

We laughed - it was always comfortable with Caitlin. The room was really starting to bend and the lights were taking on an intensity of their own now. I wasn't sure if it was the cocktail or the illicit penguin. A couple were dancing in a space that had now become a makeshift dance floor. They seemed very in tune with each other, rhythmically moving in the neon half light, looking each other in the eye as their bodies entwined then separated in perfect motion. They seemed at one with the music, expressing their souls in a way I could only dream of doing. I was tempted to get up there and perform the 'Dad Dance' for my own amusement but found myself hypnotised by their silky moves.

'Are you feeling the effects of that penguin?' I asked Caitlin, her eyes had taken on an electric blue opacity making them even more intriguing than normal.

'Not yet, takes a while to kick in' she said, waving a dismissive hand through the air.

We chatted some more and furnished our bodies with the remaining jug of purple turtle. The ice bar had become another world that was happening around us and I felt like we were having an out of body experience.

'You want to go someplace else? Before we freeze our bits off?' asked Caitlin.

'Sure, what have you got in mind?'

'I figure that when the chips are down, you just need to concentrate your mind on something else that takes your thoughts away from the problem, a bit like meditation. Come on, let's go' she replied and with that grabbed my hand and we left the neon ice world behind.

The daylight hit me like a large halibut around the face, in the subdued light of the ice bar you could be forgiven for thinking it was in fact the evening. The street looked bright, busy and the buildings loomed over me but for some reason looked as though they had a rubber consistency. People's movements were leaving trails behind them and everything looked as it did on a poor quality internet stream. The world looked a very different place in this altered reality. Caitlin began to weave again through the milling pedestrians and I attempted to mirror the trails she had left in her wake, it all felt like a computer game. I wasn't sure if I was high on drink, drugs or both. I had no idea where we were going now, much like my current predicament I was on a path to a place only God was aware of.

Caitlin headed into an amusement arcade and headed for some stairs that led down to a lower floor. The lighting was fairly ambient and the only real sounds were the gentle hum of the games machines and the sound of youths tapping away on the various buttons. She headed straight for an arcade game with a driver's seat, steering wheel and the open road on the screen ahead of her.

'You take this one' she motioned towards the adjacent driver's seat. It appeared the two of us could race each other on separate screens. I lowered myself into the bucket style seat and we put a pound in each.

'It's just you and the steering wheel Tim, let everything else go and just concentrate on winning the race' she instructed.

'Okay I'll give it a go' I said, wondering quite what I was doing at my age.

The race was about to start, I revved the engine and a surprisingly satisfying roar emanated from the sound speaker on the side of the arcade game. The countdown began and suddenly the race was underway. I sped around the first bend and clipped another car, the whole seat shook with the simulated impact and it felt strangely realistic. I dodged another collision and then saw a yellow name above the car in front, it was Caitlin. We were in the same race and this seemed to bring out my competitive streak.

'Whoa I'm catching you up!' I said, staring intently at the screen as I swerved and skidded around the next bend, hanging on to her by the coat tails. The other cars were all computer opponents but it added to the realism having additional opponents in the race. I managed to slip down the inside lane and at the next bend overtook Caitlin who was becoming quite vocal next to me. The race had taken on an entirely new meaning as we became more and more immersed in this pixel laden world. Nothing else mattered at that moment, we simply had to drive to the best of our ability and the grand prize would be to finish higher than the other person, whether it was for bragging rights I couldn't be sure. But it was an immersive experience, in that brief moment I had forgotten about the redundancy, Irene, the lack of success in the job arena and my impending financial meltdown. Winning this race was my sole purpose. We entered the final lap and the competition was reaching a roaring crescendo, the climax was just around the corner. The tyres screeched as our cars swung around various texture mapped corners and I left the other racers in my wake as I prepared to take the glory. Caitlin however had other plans and was suddenly alongside me on the screen, ramming my car in an attempt to throw me off course. We shouted and cajoled each other as the black and white finishing line appeared and it was neck and neck as we reached it. There was an ominous pause as the screen took an eternity to calculate the result, every millisecond felt like an hour. I could feel my heart thumping from the adrenaline and then it finally announced the winner.

'You jammy bastard - beginners luck! Best of three?' she virtually shouted.

'I don't have any coins on me, just this twenty'

'That will cover it, I'll go get some change' she replied as she took the note and disappeared off to the change machine. She returned with a tower of gold coins and stacked them up on the flat plastic between our two seats.

'Round two' she announced, slipping the coins in.

We raced again like possessed demons, losing all track of time as we became fully immersed in the experience. Caitlin won the second race and immediately put more coins in. We raced again and again and this continued with us shouting and cajoling each other, to all intents and purposes we were in our own world. Finally the coin tower had reduced to nothing and we looked at each other.

'Shall we play again?' I asked. Caitlin was looking around the room.

'Erm...I'm not sure that's a good idea'

'Why? What's the problem?' I enquired then noticed that we were being stared at by a selection of onlookers who were literally gazing open mouthed in our direction. At that point the realisation hit both of us that we had been shouting progressively louder and had become more and more manic as time had passed. This unusual behaviour hadn't gone entirely unnoticed.

'Do you think we should go?' I suggested.

'Fuck it, let's give them something to really stare at' came the reply. With that I threw another pound into the waiting slot and we carried on unabated.

After whiling away the afternoon in the basement of the arcades we spilled out into the streets, laughing like children at our misdemeanour. The looks on the faces of the other gamers had been priceless and was something I imagined we would laugh about for some time. I became conscious of the phone vibrating in my pocket however I was having such a good day I didn't want to spoil it by reintroducing reality into the mix. The working day was drawing to a close and the city would soon be awash with hordes of corporate drones who had endured a much less entertaining day than mine. The very world I had wished for seemed momentarily further away than it had ever been and the worrying thing was, I didn't feel like I cared for it.

'Do you need to get going?' she asked.

'I should but I really can't deal with Rachel and that mad woman right now' I responded.

'I know where we can go' she replied with a twinkle in her eye.

We headed for the tube again and after another short trip found ourselves on the outskirts of town in semi suburbia. I felt much more at home in this environment.

'Dare I ask where we're going?'

'You'll see, we just have a bit of walking to do. Are you hungry?'

'Okay, I could do with something to eat in all honesty'

'Wait there' she instructed as we approached a convenience store. A few minutes later she emerged with a bag and continued walking to this unknown destination. The sun was starting to dip now and the haze of early evening was forming, the sky a golden red with all the promise of a sunny day in the pipeline for the next day. We turned into an alley with tall conifer bushes lining one side of the path and an incredibly high wall on the other. After a few minutes of walking Caitlin slowed down and appeared to be looking for something in the bushes.

'Through here' she motioned, pointing at the bush.

'Say what now? Why are we going through a bloody bush?'

It was too late though as she had already pushed though the tightly knitted bushes and was gone, bar the scent of her perfume. In the true spirit of fuck-it Friday I squeezed through the bushes and wondered what on earth was in store on the other side. Caitlin looked at me and chuckled to herself at my less than gracious attempt to pass through as I practically fell out of the foliage. We were now stood in the grounds of some sort of building that looked to all intents and purposes like a cross between a normal building and a castle. There were lots of bushes dotted around and the markings of a football pitch towards the rear of the expansive garden. There were various strange statues and a large sundial in close proximity to the building itself.

'I'm sorry, but what are we doing here? We're trespassing for one thing' I couldn't help but ask.

'There's no actual law against trespassing Tim. When was the last time you heard of someone being prosecuted for it?'

she reasoned.

'Now you come to mention it....' I really couldn't recall ever hearing of it.

'This way, but keep to the edge of the bushes' she warned, then began edging towards the building.

'What is this place?'

'It's a private school but I love the fact it has turrets and battlements like a castle, how cool is that?'

'I don't know what to say, I guess it's pretty cool' I replied, perplexed.

We approached the rear of the building and there in front of us was a wrought iron external staircase that appeared to lead up to the top of the building. I shot Caitlin a look.

'Are you serious?'

'Come on Tim, it will be worth your while' she promised demurely.

I glanced up at the iron staircase and with a sense of trepidation duly followed as Caitlin strode ahead towards the top. Not keen on heights it became somewhat concerning as we approached the peak and the thought occurred I would have to look down before the descent. The steps opened out onto a flat piece of roof surrounded by knee-high battlements and a variety of turrets and skylights revealing rooms below. As I passed one of the raised skylights I spotted a person in the room below.

'Caitlin there's a fucking person in there! You didn't mention people would still be here?!'

'Keep it down then Tim or they'll know we're up here'.

We made our way along the top of the building, weaving around the raised skylights and then Caitlin sat down on a sloping tiled roof section that housed one of the rooms below.

'A little known secret' she whispered looking over my shoulder. I turned around to see the most amazing view of the city, every landmark and prominent building you could think of nestled into one definitive collection, bathed in the golden warm glow of the setting sun.

'Wow, the city looks unreal from up here'

'This is where I come to get a different perspective on things. Beauty can be found in hidden places, it's also a great place to come down from the high, get some mellow time. Where do you go for that?'

'You come down from a high by climbing up somewhere high?'

'Kind of ironic I know'

'I'll be honest I seek solace from the depths of a whisky glass, I don't tend to get high' I conceded.

'Did you enjoy the penguin?' she asked.

'I've had a great time - I would never have done any of these things if that course hadn't been cut short. I didn't expect to see you again, I'm so glad we met today'

'Not least in a penguin suit' she chuckled. The sun's diminishing rays gave her light blue eyes a translucent appearance as they twinkled in the half light. In that moment I realised that feelings I had long since buried may have resurfaced, like a long lost relative. Not that I could afford any further confusion in my life at this time. She emptied the contents of the carrier bag and revealed some cans of beer, crisps and a selection of nuts. Our rooftop terrace had now been transformed into a bar.

'How did you find the altered state of consciousness?' she asked, breaking the hypnotic trance I had succumbed to.

'Everything seemed like a dream, I have never felt so in tune with the world yet so detached at the same time. Although I did feel like I could achieve anything if I put my mind to it' I replied honestly.

'I had a message from my flatmate a little while back, I'm afraid those penguins were just bits of paper.' she admitted whilst handing over a freshly opened beer.

'What the fuck? But I was high! And I felt like I could achieve anything, there's no way' I spluttered.

'You see how you can change your mind set with the help of a little belief. You thought you were having a trip and so allowed yourself to be immersed in the experience' she reasoned. It did make sense, but at the same time it was mind blowing to consider the day's events had not taken place in a drug induced haze, but through an altered state of my own consciousness.

'I don't know what to say to that'

'So do you see how life opens up doors if you just let it in? You can achieve anything you want if you put your mind to it'.

We sat and looked out onto the dimly lit vista as we came down from the bits of paper we'd eaten earlier. The sun's fading rays rested across the top edges of the city skyline as she cast her final rites for another day.

I arrived home far later than ever before, having said my goodbyes to Caitlin and finally exchanging numbers. What an extraordinary day it had been and it was surprising how I had allowed myself to be led into a world of ice bars, drugs (albeit fake), arcade racing and trespassing on the rooftop of a castle-like school to watch the sunset. But for all that, it had been the most exhilarating day I could remember for quite some time. The experience made me think about how my outlook could influence my behaviour and the potential resultant outcomes. It had given me renewed optimism for the quest that was lying ahead.

'Tim why didn't you answer your phone, where the hell have you been?' asked an irate Rachel as I entered the house.

'I was taken away by a giant penguin and forced to take drugs in an ice bar' I replied. Many a truthful word said in jest.

'We're starving, you could have let me know you were running late' she rasped. Apparently I was the only person in the house capable of cooking.

'My phone battery ran out of juice this afternoon' I blurted in the absence of any logical explanation. It seemed perfectly plausible, that was until it rang in my pocket.

'How strange' I remarked staring at it in mock surprise that it was suddenly working again.

'Yes...how strange' came the sarcastic reply.

'Here's my credit card, can you order us a takeaway. Speaking of which, I've got to call the credit card company upstairs' I responded before ascending the most boring steps of the day so far. I poured a whisky and dialled the number on my latest statement. After listening to an eternal number of voice options the call eventually landed with a human being called Rakesh.

'Good evening Mr Fellows, could you just confirm some details for security?' he asked.

'Are these the same details I just answered on the keypad?'

'Can I take your date of birth please?' he answered, avoiding the question.

'I've already answered that' I replied indignantly.

'I need it for security Mr Fellows'

'Why does the automated voice ask for these details then?' I enquired.

'Just to make sure you get through to the right team, but I do have to verify them before we can look at your account'.

'By the time I've been through all these voice options and then answered your questions I will need a bigger credit limit to pay my phone bill next month' I exclaimed in frustration.

I gave date of birth, mother's maiden name, home address and hoped that was all.

'Would you like my DNA genome sequence too?' I rasped.

'No thank you sir, we don't require your gnomes' he responded. I put my head in my hands.

'Okay, I've noticed the balance transfer offer has ended, is there anything you can do with the rate as I am a long standing customer?'

'One moment Sir' I could hear some tapping in the background. This was the bit where they pretended to look into your account and then offer you an incredibly low rate for another year.

'At the moment there are no offers on your account' came the response after a while.

'Sorry, are you saying there's nothing you can do about the rate?' I was surprised.

'I'm afraid not Sir'

'But if you look back for the last seven years or so you'll see I have been given offers of around 2.9% every year. What about balance transfers?'

'There are no offers on your account' he replied.

'So what are my options?'

'You can pay the statement every month, transfer it away or pay it all off in one go'.

'But the monthly payments have rocketed now the interest rate has ended. I haven't got £600 spare every month just to cover the interest it's absolutely ridiculous!' I was becoming very concerned now.

'You could apply for our premium card which has an introductory rate of 0% for the first twelve months'

'Can you not just give me that then?'

'No you have to start a fresh new application, it can be done online'

'Right well I'll have to do that then' I replied and slammed the phone down in frustration. I was livid, years of being a loyal customer and paying my bill every month without fail seemed to count for nothing all of a sudden. I fired up the laptop. At that moment Irene popped her head around the door.

'I'm on to you' she announced, giving me a suspicious look before walking off. Sometimes, in fact most of the time, I wondered which nefarious sins I had committed in a previous incarnation to warrant this form of purgatory bestowed upon me.

I decided to perform some web based research to investigate if other customers of my credit card company had experienced the sudden inexplicable withdrawal of offers. Sure enough there was tale after tale of the same thing happening. There seemed to be quite a few forums and worryingly I stumbled upon articles from financial websites alluding to the fact that these credit card companies had run a report to determine the customers that may have represented a risk. It went on to say that once identified, these customers would effectively be frozen out of any attractive offers and forced to either settle up, move their debt away or declare insolvency. The bastards were trying to protect their own enormous arses now that the economic climate had taken a turn for the worse. I did the maths and realised they had my number. I had a fairly large mortgage, sizeable credit card debt and only one income. I felt an incredible panic at that moment and could only hope that my strong credit score and previous good payment history would stand me in good stead for their premier credit card application. Otherwise I didn't know what else I could do.

I ventured onto their website and filled out the online application, which was a trial in itself as they wanted to know endless minutia. Then I came to the employment section and it dawned on me that I was not in a position to name an employer, unless I accidently used my former employer's details. I sat and stared at the form whilst contemplating my predicament. The stark reality was that I wouldn't be accepted for credit anywhere whilst not employed. Did I want to commit fraud and lie on the application form? It was a moral dilemma and the thought of spending years behind bars weighed heavily in favour of not lying on the form. As much as I knew it was unintentional, I felt like the credit card company had known about the redundancy and seen their chance to squeeze me into furnishing their deeply lined pockets with it. At that moment my phone started ringing again, it was Richard Long. Of course it was, immaculate timing as always. I was aware of someone ascending the stairs and heading towards the room.

'Dinner has arrived Tim, are you going to come down and dish up?' asked Rachel. I assumed it was a rhetoric question as I wouldn't have expected her to risk injury serving the food I had paid for all of us to eat. I closed the laptop and my head was spinning with the problem of the credit card. The only realistic option I could conceivably see was to pay off the card in full and then only spend what I needed until I found a new job. Otherwise the redundancy payout would soon be eaten by the monthly interest. That did represent an element of risk but I could see the money gradually disappearing otherwise and then I would be left with an enormous credit card bill and sizeable mortgage with nothing coming in to pay for it. Everything would be lost. Damn the bloody credit crunch and everything it stood for.

First Impressions

I awoke several times in the night after eventually achieving sleep in the first place. It had become increasingly harder to relax at night as events played on my mind. I stared around the room at the dimly lit walls and furnishings, faced with the realisation that all of it could be taken away in a flash. It was a strange feeling after years of having no reason to even think about the longevity of my home and possessions. Now I looked at them as if I didn't deserve them. Rachel was fast asleep next to me - our predicament was clearly having no effect on her ability to relax at night. When I looked back on over the years I knew in my heart that things had always been awkward between us. The night I proposed should have been a sign. I had carried out the appropriate research and notified the restaurant in advance that I was planning to pop the question. The waiter had shown us to our seats, taken our order and retreated into the background. I had been aware of them looking over which added to the growing tension I'd felt. Rachel had knocked her fork onto the floor and I duly knelt down to retrieve it and handed it back to her. In an instant the waiter had returned with two glasses of champagne and began congratulating us both and proceeded to shake my hand furiously. Then he realised the shiny object she held was a piece of cutlery and I had no option other than to propose in front of the entire restaurant who were already spectators. He was very apologetic afterwards.

Rain was beating against the window panes, before

making the journey south towards the sills and dripping onto the waiting flower beds outside. To my surprise I could actually hear the sound of each drop as it collected and then made the leap of faith onto the geraniums. Although to my mind it sounded more like it was hitting wood. Listening more intently the realisation came to me in a moment of horror. The water was indeed landing on wood.

'The bloody roof's leaking!' I shrieked, leaping out of bed like a man possessed. Rachel sat bolt upright and looked completely confused, having been rudely awakened from her deep slumber.

'Seriously? You better get a bucket' was all she could say.

'Great timing, why does it have to wait until now its had years to do this' I muttered as I went in search of a bucket. They said it never rained it just poured and at that moment it was literally doing so in my house. As I made my way down the stairs I noticed there was a light coming from the living room and I could hear some tapping noises emanating from inside along with the gentle thrum of the television. My mind was racing at this point and at least I could rule out a burglary, as they tended not to watch television to the best of my knowledge. I peered into the room and there was Irene in all her naked glory sat in front of the television with the phone to one ear.

'I think I've got it this time' she remarked, gesturing towards the screen.

'Got what exactly?' I asked.

'The solution to that puzzle' she announced looking pleased with herself. I looked at the screen and she was watching a late night quiz program that invited the viewer to call the show and try to answer the impossible riddle on the screen. To my horror I noticed the premium rate number in big red letters on the screen and the mention of calls costing £1 a minute. Irene had been sitting up at night calling these premium numbers at my expense! I was absolutely livid. I tried to take the earpiece from her but she had hold of it in a vice-like grip and snarled at me like a rabid St Bernard. So I cancelled the call and unplugged the phone at the socket. The last thing I needed on top of the fence, roof and lack of job was Irene costing me more unnecessary money. I couldn't even make her pay the phone bill.

'That's enough Irene you do realise these shows are a massive con' I said in an exasperated tone.

'You are a massive con Tim, at least I'm trying to bring some money into this sinking ship' she rebuffed with all the nonchalance of a teenager who thought they were never in the wrong.

'Yes but you do realise it's costing a fortune and the probability of winning is very low Irene' I was too tired to take offence at this early hour.

'Are you bringing this bucket Tim?' Rachel shouted from upstairs. I decided to ignore her.

'Could you please wear pyjamas or even a dressing gown around the house if you're going to wander around at night. It's not really fair exposing yourself to all and sundry. It isn't fair on Ellen either' I felt a weight come off as I finally plucked up the courage to tackle this issue. She frowned and looked me up and down before her gaze rested uncomfortably upon my nether regions. I looked down and there it was, Timothy Junior was hanging out of the slip at the front of my pyjama shorts. Of course it was - just as I had tried to exert some authority over the troublesome woman. She always seemed to have the last laugh.

'Just go to bed Irene' I conceded before skulking off to the kitchen to fetch a bucket. After rummaging around for a while I eventually found the bucket in its latest hiding place and returned to the bedroom to catch the water dripping from the ceiling. I observed the front room was now in darkness as I ascended the stairs, half expecting the ceiling to have given way to a view of the sky above. Luckily that wasn't the case.

'You'll have to get someone in to look at the roof first thing tomorrow'

'Thank you for imparting your wisdom' I replied without

thinking first. She could always be relied upon to state the obvious at the most annoying moment. I positioned the bucket under the trajectory of the dripping water and returned to bed, although Rachel seemed to have taken over my side for some reason. The sound of water droplets hitting wood had been replaced with them landing in the bucket instead, which was no less annoying.

'We could, you know....as we're both awake now' I suggested cheekily, stroking Rachel's arm. Her skin felt quite dry, it didn't usually feel like that. I noticed she had a lavender scent about her, which wasn't a favourite of hers either. I leapt out of bed as if it was ablaze and switched the light on. My worst fears were confirmed by the sight of Irene lying on my side of the bed. The woman was a menace! It was no use, I decided instead to go downstairs and ponder the meaning of my weary existence instead. Rachel had clearly gone back to sleep and was unaware of the whole incident.

I awoke with a start in the armchair, the house was alive with activity and night had turned into day. I must have fallen asleep in the front room.

'Enjoy your lie-in?' Rachel asked.

'What time is it?'

'10.15 I assume you came down here as the water was dripping on the bed' she fumed.

'It wasn't above the bed' I replied, confused.

'When I woke up your side of the bed was soaked. Thanks for just leaving me in it' she replied, before exiting the house, not forgetting to slam the door in the process. I already knew what to expect as I made my way upstairs. There was no sign of water ingress above the bed and spookily it was where Irene had been laying. I surveyed the water bucket and the carnage on the bed and felt a growing feeling of despair. Somehow I sensed today would not be as much fun as yesterday. I considered messaging Caitlin to see if she fancied another day of abandonment but I knew that time was running out and I needed to knuckle down. It was very frustrating being referred to the internet at every turn as that seemed to be an easy way of ignoring people. However the thought occurred to me to try out some of the methods suggested on the course. I would target employers I wished to work for instead, make myself known to them. It had to be worth a try - after all I had nothing to lose apart from my house.

I spent a couple of hours sorting out the bedroom and arranging for a roofing contractor to come out and assess the damage. To my horror, even some of the roofing firms had multiple voice options before I could speak to an actual person. I drew up a list of potential employers, printed out CV's and prepared to hit them right between the eyes like an exocet missile. A renewed sense of optimism had presented itself, although I was conscious this wasn't the first time. The whole redundancy experience had proved to be a bit of a rollercoaster of emotions, one day I felt positive and the next downhearted and lost in a hopeless chasm of despair. Irene's declining health had started to become a real concern and I felt that Rachel was in denial as to the extent of the problem. She was starting to represent a danger to the house and I was becoming reluctant to leave her alone for long periods. Nonetheless I had to try something otherwise the job hunting would be limited to another fruitless day of being ignored by the world wide web.

As the bus meandered through the densely packed city my head was spinning with thoughts of the credit card and the overall situation I found myself in. I wasn't sure if it was my imagination but even more homes appeared to be boarded up than the previous day. Perhaps it was just because I was focusing on it more intently. I imagined my own house with these boards and the neighbours looking on shaking their heads. It was alright for them, they all still had their jobs and comfortable lives. Again my thoughts turned to

Caitlin and the fun we'd had, it was a welcome distraction from the reality of my predicament. But one thing that had been impressed upon me was the fact I was able to influence my own mind set with a little belief. I was convinced I had taken an illicit narcotic and this made me perceive the world differently for a short period. If I could just tap into that self belief a little more it could help me in my quest. Another encouraging aspect was the steely determination I felt when competing with Caitlin at the arcades. That competitive streak had taken a leave of absence for some time and it surprised and excited me at the same time to discover I still had the latent desire to be the best. It was fair to say the whole redundancy had made me question a few things about myself and at the moment the answers were not entirely forthcoming. I looked at my phone and considered messaging Caitlin again and after staring at it for a minute or two decided against it. She was probably busy anyway and I feared it would be hard to top the events of yesterday. I still felt drawn to her in ways I couldn't explain and at this moment the luxury of thinking about it was not affordable. Another reason I needed to find employment was my decreasing patience with public transport, sat around with the sort of people who believed an archipelago to be some form of bird.

I arrived in town with my hit list of preferred employers and tried to recite the teachings from the course. We were told to show up in person and enquire about vacancies. Also we had to appear frequently at these prospective employers for various reasons, the idea being our faces would seem familiar when it came to gaining an interview. I liked that idea and could see how it would work in a subliminal way. The day was overcast and the office blocks seemed to tower over me again, but I was determined to make the best of it and put my best foot forward, whatever that meant. They both looked the same to me.

The first on my list was Lindus International Ltd, whose offices were situated on the outskirts of town in an imposing block with the obligatory revolving doors adorning the entrance. I approached the building and adopted a confident walk, nodding to a gentleman who was exiting the building as I prepared to enter. He looked at me as if I was on some kind of spectrum. I breezed into the reception and made my way purposefully towards the desk, behind which two ladies were seated. One hawk-like woman was busy looking at her mobile phone and the other was staring intently at a social media website. I thought for a moment I was invisible to them as to my surprise they made no attempt to communicate.

'Good morning I wonder if you could help me' I offered. The one that looked like a hawk broke her mobile phone activity and looked up in apparent annoyance at my temerity, daring to interrupt the pressing matter of texting whoever it was.

'Do you have an appointment?' she asked.

'No I see you are a successful international company and I would like to offer my CV for any vacancies you might have at the moment'

'Oh, okay I will take that thank you' she reached out a hand, her nails were like talons. I was worried she might shred the CV with them. She took the CV and said nothing.

'So...do you have any vacancies at the moment?' I asked. She looked surprised that I was still there.

'Nothing at the moment what was it you wanted to do specifically?'

'Ideally sales however I am open to suggestion at the moment'

'I'll put this with the others and we'll keep it on file, if anything comes up we'll contact you' she replied, before getting up and pulling a large file brimming with paperwork from the cabinet behind. The file was marked 'CV's July' and was overflowing already with a plethora of them. Worryingly it was only a few days into the month and already they had been deluged with CV's from other job seekers. I wondered what had happened to the June file.

'Thank you' I replied.

'If you look at our website you will see any new vacancies as they arise' she offered in a statement that rolled off the tongue in parrot-like fashion. I sensed she had said this a thousand times. The futility of looking at websites was really starting to frustrate me, but I managed to exercise some decorum and refrain from showing any contempt.As I left the building I pondered how to re-appear and embed my face into their world by turning up for a variety of different reasons. I realised this may need some creativity on my part and set about thinking how to achieve this. The main challenge would be to get visibility in the building and make sure that as many people saw me as possible.

I spent the rest of the day visiting other establishments in the local area and was met with similar disinterested responses from receptionists who would rather be looking at social media than providing an efficient front of house presence for their respective companies. I had to remember not to be disheartened as taking the CV's to different companies was just the first part of the master plan. The difference between me and the other CV droppers was that I would become a familiar face and therefore when invited for interview they would feel I fitted in straight away. I caught the bus back home, considerably earlier than the previous day in an attempt to rebuild some bridges with the disgruntled Rachel. She was somewhat frosty when I returned, although this was starting to become normal. I was more concerned if she appeared friendly or affectionate. That behaviour usually precipitated a request to splash money we could ill afford on an amazing item that represented the missing piece of the jigsaw. Whatever the proposed addition was, it would invariably paper over the cracks for a short period of time. I felt sad that I saw my marriage in that light as it hadn't always been like that. Or had it? Maybe I had just become accustomed to thinking there was something magical about it in the early days as a way of justifying it to myself. The trouble was, I couldn't put my hand on my heart and honestly say one way or the other. Until recently I had a good job and was content with my home life, now I found myself questioning everything, it was all very disconcerting and confusing. I just wanted everything to revert to normal again. Seeing Caitlin had added more confusion to the mix, as I felt a certain magnetism to her and I knew deep down there was no way I could spend regular time in her company, Rachel wouldn't just say 'Yes of course you can go to the cinema with that attractive fun loving female friend of yours'. Then of course I needed to make a decision about the credit card. Again I knew I had little choice other than to pay it back as the interest was so high. It occurred to me I could pay it back and then just use it in extreme emergencies until I found another job. It represented a bit of a gamble and some would say a monumental one, of Empire State Building proportions. I was still reeling from the shock of their attitude but what else could I do? They had me over a barrel and were preparing to insert something terrible as I flailed around helplessly.

I logged onto my online credit card account and paid the majority of the balance, leaving enough for me to get by on for a month. I figured this would pressurize me into action, when the going got tough Tim Fellows got going. Or Tim Fellows would be gone, depending on the outcome. I tortured myself for a short while looking despairingly at the large amount of money languishing in my account, before pressing the button to transfer it to the leeches that were my credit card company. In an instant, it was gone – the most amount of money I had ever had to my name was now the property of an organisation that had screwed me over to protect themselves. I knew deep down it was my fault getting into debt in the first place but did they really have to force me to the wall at this particular time? It was the timing more than anything that had got to me. Not only had I lost my job they were intent on turning the screw to try and really cause me a problem. I shut the laptop and trudged dejectedly downstairs to join the dinner table, although in truth I wasn't really very hungry. On the one hand it was a relief to finally pay off the debt that had been hanging over me like a giant vampire bat for years but on the other hand I felt daunted by the challenge that lie ahead.

'When is the roofer coming?' asked Rachel in her iciest manner possible.

'Thursday morning' I responded.

'I hope it doesn't rain again before then' she sniped.

'The forecast is good for the next few days' I lied.

'Have you got a job yet? Was that training course useful?'

'Yes the course was very enlightening, I learnt a great deal' I replied, there was a double meaning to my response. Irene looked at me in a disapproving way.

'Training courses don't work, if you need proof of that just look at him' Irene announced pointing an accusing finger in my general direction. I was speechless. More concerning was the fact Rachel didn't even acknowledge the comment. Was this a commonly held view in the house?

'Thank you for your input Irene, from now on perhaps your role in this conversation could be a silent one' I said sarcastically.

'You need to network more' she replied.

'I'm sorry I didn't realise you were such an expert. Please do go ahead and give us all the benefit of your undisputed wisdom' I couldn't contain my sarcasm.

'You need to get on social media'

'Do you even know what that is?'

'Of course I do. How do you think I met Eddie?'

'Who the hell is Eddie?'

At that moment an elderly gentleman resembling Albert Einstein walked into our kitchen diner and offered his wizened hand in an attempt to shake mine.

'Pleased to meet you Tim, thank you for the invite to dinner' he croaked.

'Erm….hello Eddie…you're welcome' I muttered, truly astonished that my house had now become a romantic rendezvous for the elderly. I shot Rachel a look and she just stared blankly back at me.

'Irene tells me you can't get a job' said Eddie.

'I am currently looking for work yes' I replied. Apparently I was now answerable to anyone who walked in off the street.

'Do you miss your old job?' he asked.

'Yes, I'm afraid I really do' I replied. It struck me that he was the first person to ask that question.

'You need to stay friendly with them, in case a vacancy comes up at your old company' he advised.

'Maybe, I'm just a little aggrieved by the manner in which it was all dealt with'

'You need to get over yourself Tim. Get them round for dinner' Irene stated.

'Thank you all for your advice' I replied, losing the will to live.

'You'll need a job to support us if Eddie and I have a baby' announced Irene. I looked at him and he smiled unflinchingly. Christ on a bike, he was also away with the fairies. But something they had said did actually resonate with me. Maybe I should invite my former colleagues over one for an evening of food and merriment - I made a mental note to do so. But first I had to begin phase two of the master plan of making myself known to the companies I had visited earlier today.

After sleeping reasonably well I made the daily pilgrimage into town and headed straight for Lindus International's building. It was essential I was seen around the building by as many people as possible so that my face 'fitted' subconsciously when it came to the all-important interview. This was subject to being lucky enough to get an interview of course. I strode with conviction to the front desk and noticed a raft of visitors gathered around the area. This was the perfect opportunity, I would just merge into the throng and follow them past the gatekeepers and then I had free access to the building. With expert stealth moves I slowly edged toward them and then just as they peeled away from the receptionists I used them as a shield and casually walked alongside them before heading for the stairs. I felt a rush of adrenaline at this new found bravery and suspected the day with Caitlin had reignited a dormant reckless streak that had become constrained by responsibility over recent years. This was much more like the Tim Fellows of old, taking risks in order to get where he wanted to go. Maybe that was why I felt drawn to the mercurial Caitlin - she had an unpredictable streak and vivacious personality that meant no two days were the same. Rachel on the other hand was often cold and distant, apparently consumed by her own narcissism to such a degree that anything outside of that was deemed insignificant. I would've liked to spend a day in either Rachel or Irene's world just to experience a total detachment from the reality for a short while. It made me wonder if the reason men had shorter life expectancies was primarily because they were run into the ground by the women in their lives. I realised that was not a very diverse or politically correct view in the modern world but it crossed my mind nonetheless. In reality it was probably just different attitudes to stress coupled with genetics and lifestyle I reasoned.

I passed a gentleman on the stairs and nodded in his direction as if I knew him, he returned the gesture to my surprise. So that was one person who had registered my presence and accepted it. This was easier than I thought. Taking confidence I decided to venture onto one of the floors and really promote my face to the workforce. I entered a large open plan area, much like my former workplace. Employees were dotted around the floor - some were staring intently at their screens typing furiously as if their lives depended on it. Others were on the phone gesticulating with their hands as if the person at the end of the phone could see them. Three ladies were gathered around one monitor, trawling through a colleague's holiday photo's on the internet. There was a gentle buzz about the place and I wished I had a legitimate reason to be there. One day maybe I might have one. I walked around the floor saying hello to people, some responded, others look baffled. Either way I had made an impression on them and that was the purpose of the exercise. Any one of those people could be interviewing me in the not to distant future. It amazed me that nobody challenged my presence in the building.

'Sorry can I help you?' sounded an inquisitive voice to my right. I turned round to see a portly man wielding a dangerous looking moustache.

'No thanks I'm down from Head Office, just finding my way around'. I replied.

'This is Head Office' he responded.

'Just my little joke' I replied whilst tying not to look horrified at my faux pas.

'Are you an IT contractor?' he enquired.

'Yes that's right' I seized upon the opportunity, as IT contractors often wandered around offices appearing bemused in my experience. I started to feel a little uncomfortable with the lying but knew I had to appear confident or the façade would come crashing down,

'Be a good sport and give this to Ian, it's for the video conference' he offered a grey webcam and I dutifully took it, after all I would be seeing Ian when I finally located him.

'Sure thing, I haven't seen him for a while, have you?'

'Yes he was on the third floor doing an install' was the response.

'Great I'll catch up with him there then' I replied. At least I now knew where to find him. I left the rotund moustache bearer and weaved in and out of the array of desks and partitioned areas, saying hello to as many people as possible. I saw a couple of people at the printer so I joined the queue in an attempt to appear like I belonged in their lives. There was a young man and slightly older lady at the printer engaged in work related conversation.

'Printer's not working upstairs again' I said, pretending to be annoyed about it. Perhaps I should've been an actor. Plenty of them seem to have made careers out of playing themselves.

'This one is playing up too' replied the lady. She sported an officious appearance and was peering at me over her glasses.

'That's okay he works in IT' came a voice from behind me, it was the man from a moment ago. All eyes were on me.

'What seems to be the problem with this one?' I stupidly asked, knowing nothing about printers.

'It says there is no network configured but we've been using it already this morning' announced the young man, pointing at the machine.

'Ah right okay, let me have a look at it' I found myself saying, as they made way for me. I pressed the most obvious settings on the display panel and scrolled through the various options, nodding periodically and muttering to myself as if I was working from a checklist stored in the recesses of my brain. Of course there was nothing I really understood in the network configuration setting. I recalled my experience of dealing with IT professionals and decided to call upon this knowledge to solve the problem.

'Have you tried re-booting?' I asked.

'Erm, no' came the reply and the three of them looked at each other with that knowing look. I had instantly become a bona-fide IT contractor. To my surprise, it actually worked.

'Brilliant thank you, sorry I didn't catch your name?' asked the lady.

'Tim' I replied instinctively, then wondered if I should have divulged my real name. They didn't mention that on the course. But then they didn't advocate illegally infiltrating businesses either.

'I better go and find Ian' I said before walking away in the direction of the double doors.

Although it was effectively trespassing I found myself enjoying being in a workplace again. I will admit in a strange way that it felt a little odd. I looked at the employees who all seemed to be dedicated to the company and wondered if they realised how easily they might be discarded if their employer suffered a downturn in fortune. These people were all trying to climb the career ladders and I suspected had no idea what it felt like to have the rug pulled from under them. I hoped they never found out.

Growing in confidence I continued my tour of the building, making small talk with various people making sure I didn't stay in any one place too long. The more I walked around, the more information I garnered that could be used in conversation. I still received the occasional puzzled look from genuine employees but any reaction was a good one as I saw it. After consuming what felt like several litres of water at various dispensers I located the toilets and pushed the door open to reveal a swish decorated room, you could tell a lot about an employer by the condition of those areas. Everything from the walls to the cubicle doors had been colour co-ordinated. I made a mental note to find this Ian character when I reached the third floor. Looking around the room I noticed there were no urinals, which struck me as unusual. was almost as puzzling as the sound of female voices so close to the toilet door. In fact so close they sounded like they were coming in to the men's toilet. Then to my horror I realised the reason for the missing urinals was that I had inadvertently found my way into the ladies toilets. In a moment of panic I leapt into the nearest open cubicle and managed to shut the door just as they entered the room. They were in mid conversation about something called Project Rock which sounded intriguing and possibly a conversation topic I could use to enhance my fake employee status. In an attempt to hide my obviously male shoes from view I thought it best to climb atop the toilet. This needed to be completed quietly otherwise it would sound suspicious to the ladies outside. As I brought my right leg up slowly onto the toilet lid I then began to slowly retract the left one, bringing it upwards to join its counterpart. I was surprised by my dexterity, if this was ever considered an Olympic sport I would put myself forward as a competitor. For a brief second I visualised collecting the gold medal to rapturous applause, as Rachel cheered on admiringly and my mother turned to her neighbour Mrs Warburton and told her how proud she was. Slightly distracted with these thoughts of Olympic toilet seat perching I lost my footing on the edge of the seat and found myself falling forward like a one legged giraffe atop an iceberg. Everything went black as I hit either the door or the side of the cubicle, I couldn't be sure which.

'He's coming round' announced a voice from somewhere that seemed both distant and yet somehow near at the same time in my fog shrouded brain. I could feel a pounding sensation at the back of my head and something very cold and wet pressed against it. I wasn't sure who or where I was at this precise moment, or even what day it was. I could see a collection of people crouched around me looking concerned as my focus improved. Was this a dream? Would I look down and see I was only wearing a pair of boxer shorts and everyone in the room would have animal heads? Sadly it became apparent this wasn't a dream and I started to recall where I was and why I shouldn't be sitting dazed on the ladies toilet floor in a building I had no reason to be in.

'Sir, you've had a nasty fall' stated a paramedic man with a kind face.

'I don't remember' I said, not knowing what to say.

'Of course he doesn't' said a lady employee stood nearby.

'Can you remember what you were doing in the ladies toilet with this webcam?' enquired another lady who looked every inch like the archetypal boss. I realised this didn't look good at all and just stared blankly, hiding behind the veil of the rapidly dispersing vagueness.

'We need to take you to the hospital you may have concussion' said the paramedic. I was helped to my feet and holding the ice pack in place I followed the paramedic out of the ladies toilet. The lights seemed very bright and the room was spinning a little, it reminded me of the day with Caitlin. As we entered the main office floor the magnitude of the situation quickly became apparent as the majority of the company were staring at me. I could see an array of faces, looking at me as if I was a previously undiscovered life form that had been teleported from the planet Zargos. Some were shaking their heads and others muttering under their breath as I took the walk of shame past them all. It felt like the longest walk in the history of man as I made my way out of the building with my entourage. I caught the sound of an onlooker using the word 'pervert' and heard other adjectives bandied about with the utmost contempt. As I was led out of the building and into the waiting paramedic's car I looked up at the building in dismay. I had wanted to make my face known to them and had certainly succeeded on an epic scale.

Opportunity Knocks

After a lengthy period of waiting at the Accident and Emergency area at the local hospital I had finally been discharged and sent home with a bandage around my head and a selection of painkillers. I could have bought all of the items from the chemist in a matter of minutes, rather than hanging around with the sick and wounded for hours. The paramedic had mentioned that Lindus may well contact the police and that I should expect a call imminently. Just what I didn't need, how was I going explain this latest out of character episode to Rachel? I wondered if my slow descent into madness had even registered. I had barely noticed how quickly I had changed from a responsible nine to five citizen into a drug taking trespassing lunatic. I decided I needed to return myself to some form of normality and the sooner the better. I contacted some of the guys from my old office while I was languishing in the waiting area and arranged for them to come over for a dinner party of sorts. As I trudged out of the automatic hospital doors I made eye contact with a face that seemed familiar. The other person also appeared to recognise me and there was a brief pause where we both weighed up the possibility of engaging with the other. It was too late, we had committed.

'Tim?' asked the smartly dressed dark haired man.

'Yes erm...'

'It's me, David from school' he quickly filled in the blanks for me.

'Ah yes, fancy seeing you here'

'I work here in R&D' he explained.

'Is that Ruptures and Dismemberment?' I quipped.

'Still got your old sense of humour I see' he exclaimed.

'It's the one thing they can't take'

'Who are they?' he asked, sensing there was more to my statement than a standard cliché.

'The mortgage company, I was made redundant and trying to find another job is proving as challenging as building a Porsche out of an inner tube, some chicken bone and a roll of wire'

'Oh I'm sorry to hear that old chap' he sympathised, as much as men have the capacity to do so.

'Yes I put the best years of my working life into that firm and this is the thanks I get'

'It's a sign of the times Tim' he conceded then suddenly it seemed he had hit upon an idea.

'I tell you what - if you're interested in earning some money I'm always looking for people to undergo clinical trials. Nothing heavy duty it's just trying out sleeping pills and that kind of thing'.

'Sure, I am open to suggestion at this stage, every little helps' I found myself saying.

'If you've got a minute I just need you to fill out a form and we can get you started.'

'Sure why not'

'Splendid buddy, in that case follow me to my office'. He instructed and we made our way through the myriad of corridors.

'Have you got anything for anxiety?' I asked half joking.

'As it happens yes, these are similar to beta blockers but also have the added benefit of lowering cholesterol. They are a new wave of super drug that look after your heart in more ways than one. I will give you some to take away and a review form. I will need you to sign a disclaimer though.'

I wondered what I was now getting myself into, but it was nice to feel even slightly employed.

'So other than the redundancy, how is life working out for you?' enquired David.

'I've been married to Rachel for years and we have a daughter Ellen. What about yourself?'

'Brilliant, it sounds like you've been busy. A life of

medicine has taken most of my time, thirty hour shifts take their toll. I have met someone I like but it's difficult to move things forward, I'm not very experienced in that area' he conceded.

'Yes I think these things usually happen organically' I replied as if I knew. At that moment I wondered how I would tell Caitlin how I felt if the situation should ever present itself. Not that I was in a position to consider such things.

'I might need to tap you up for some advice Tim' he replied.

'I'll try and help you if I can' I replied, after all it was the least I could do.

Returning home was becoming a part of the day I had started to dread. It seemed to involve me having to fabricate stories in order to cover up events that I could never tell Rachel. It also caused my anxiety to increase just being in the house, not helped by Irene's increasingly erratic behaviour. I wondered if it hadn't been for Ellen if I would ever be in this situation now out of choice. It was a terrible thought and I immediately discarded it, giving myself a stern talking to in the process. I could see there was activity in the hall as I approached the front door although I couldn't make out what was happening through the frosted glass. Turning the key in the lock I opened the door and there was Rachel and Irene scrubbing the walls furiously. They both stopped in their tracks and just stared at me like a pair of foxes looking down the barrel into the eyes of an armed hunter. Either that or they were wondering why my head was adorned with a bandage. It was the latter.

'Oh my God what have you done to your head?' asked Ellen, who had appeared in the hall. She ran towards me and gave me a big hug.

'Did you have a nice time at the camp?' I asked trying to deflect the attention. Irene and Rachel were still staring as if they'd been paused by some sort of operator with a remote control. I would like to have one of those remote controls I mused.

'Yes Daddy I will tell you all about it. I've missed you' she replied.

'I've missed you too darling' I responded truthfully. It was so good to see her friendly face. In fact it had blinded me to the activities of Rachel and Irene momentarily.

'Do you promise not to be mad with Nan?' Ellen asked innocently.

'Of course I won't be mad' I replied with another Oscar winning performance.

'She was just trying to help with the decorating'

'But we aren't doing any decorating' I replied with a deepening sense of despair.

'She has painted the walls a nice pink colour but Mummy thought she should leave it to the decorators' she explained. I was too lethargic to complain, nothing was a surprise any more with that woman. I could see paint smeared all over the wallpaper in the hall and added this to the list of repairs that were mounting.

'Of course she has' I responded and made my way towards the lounge.

'Why have you got a bandage on your head?' asked Ellen again.

'I was hit by a low flying albatross' I explained as if it was actually true.

'Daddy.....'

'I just banged my head it looks worse than it is'

'Hopefully knocked some sense into you' Irene suggested helpfully.

'Maybe you should try it' I muttered as I strode past the weary woman.

Days passed after the trespassing incident and there was nothing from the police or anyone else in connection with Webcamgate. Either they were following rigorous protocol and it was all going through the due process or they had decided not to pursue the matter. I didn't expect to hear

123

anything from them at all. That was until my phone started vibrating at the breakfast table a few days after the event.

'Tim Fellows' I answered.

'Hi is that Tim Fellows?' the female caller asked. I wondered if anyone ever listened to the first thing you said upon answering the phone. I could have answered the phone as Goatface and it would have passed unnoticed.

'Yes speaking'

'It's Sarah Northcliffe from Lindus International' announced the caller. I froze on the spot. Rachel and Irene gazed at me.

'Hello Sarah, how can I help you?' I ventured nervously.

'I was wondering if you could spare some time to come in today for a discussion' she asked. My heart was palpitating to such an extent it may have been visible to the outside world.

'Sure what sort of time?'

'How does three o'clock sound? Nothing too formal I just have a few questions and my co-director would like to speak with you'. I was acutely aware the onlookers could hear every word so I tried to retain my composure and act as if it was for a job interview.

'Yes I think I can fit that in' I replied, affording a wry smile to Rachel who looked on impassively.

'Come to reception and ask for me when you arrive, security will come and collect you' she instructed.

'See you at three' I replied, disconnecting the call.

'Is that your fancy woman?' asked Irene.

'It was an interview actually, for a prestigious international company in town' I explained. It was essentially true, except the interview related to my misdemeanours at their premises not for a vacancy. Maybe they had decided to keep it under their own jurisdiction and not involve the police. It was probably in my best interests to try and adhere to their wishes and attempt an exercise in damage limitation. My anxiety had started to increase, characterised by a pulsating sensation in the centre of my chest and it took some measured breathing to restore parity to the situation. I made a mental note to try the tablets that David had given me. I felt like I was living a double life, hardly anything Rachel thought I was doing was actually real. If she knew what I'd really been up to I had no idea how I would ever explain it. At least the swelling on my head had reduced and the bandage was no longer necessary.

It was with much trepidation that I entered the Lindus building, especially considering the last time I had been there. But this was a necessary evil and would hopefully avert a bigger crisis. I spent the bus journey racking my brain for some sensible explanation as to how I had ended up unconscious in the ladies toilets clutching a webcam in a building I had no reason to be in. It felt like a tall order and the reason for that was simple – it was one. Maybe I would get away with being incredibly vague or by feigning mental illness and hope they decided not to pursue it any further. I could only hope. Then once all of this was cleared up I could concentrate on the small matter of finding gainful employment. I approached the reception desk cautiously and announced my arrival. She motioned towards a leather seat next to a small table and some magazines and instructed me to take a seat. Every minute that passed heightened the sense of dread. Eventually the sound of heavy footsteps could be heard and a large gentleman with the signature security attire came into view. He looked me up and down as if I was vermin and without any introduction or pleasantries signalled for me to follow him. I duly followed and as we walked along the corridor my mind raced as it tried to compute a plausible excuse. Having input the details of the problem my grey cells had produced an error message and no solution. So I decided to make shit up on the spot.

'In here' the security ape ordered, waving a paw in the direction of an ornately decorated office. He shut the door behind me as I entered. An elegant lady was poised behind an expensive looking desk and she was accompanied by an older gentleman who sported more hair on his chin than the top of his head. He looked imperiously at me over his glasses.

'Thank you for coming in to see us Tim' said Sarah as she stood up to shake my hand. I returned the handshake and then bearded man also stood up and thrust his hand forward. He nearly crushed my hand and he appeared intent on removing my arm from its socket with some vigorous shaking. I wished I'd gone in hard at that point but had elected to use a softer more humble approach instead.

'No problem it was the least I could do' I offered. Beardy man raised an eyebrow.

'As I said this is just an informal chat about the situation and then depending how things progress we may take further action' advised Sarah, affording a half smile.

'Look I should explain, I have been under a lot of pressure lately. It makes you behave differently and take risks you wouldn't normally consider' I blurted.

'I'm sure you have, redundancy is very stressful' replied Sarah. Christ they knew even more about me than I realised. Perhaps they had paid someone to rifle through my household waste and compile a dossier on me.

'Yes it is, I spent twenty years at my previous company and became an expert in the Paradox system'

'Sorry what system?' enquired the man who looked as if I'd spoken in foreign tongue.

'Exactly, this is the problem' I replied turning up the palms of my hands and looking at them in despair.

'It's a complicated database that only a select few can get to grips with. I was a green belt in Paradox'.

'I'm afraid we don't use Paradox here' the man advised.

'But you would be trained on our in house systems' added Sarah.

'I'm sorry could you just run that by me again?' I asked in a state of shock.

'If successful you will be given on the job training for all of the systems we use' she explained.

'Of course.....' I mumbled as the penny dropped. They

weren't calling me in to discuss the webcam incident – they had seen my CV and were interviewing me for a job! The problem with this began to dawn on me. They clearly had no idea I was the same person escorted from the premises only days ago and the minute they unveiled me to the workforce I would be recognised and possibly prosecuted. Even if I wasn't charged the majority of my colleagues would think of me as 'that man'. It was a very disappointing reality, if only I had simply left my CV and not tried to infiltrate the building I could be going back to the house clutching a job offer. I had no choice other than to finish the interview and politely decline any offer of work, which incidentally would be the only one on the table since the wretched redundancy.

'Sorry about the security man by the way. It's just that we had an incident recently whereby an intruder was acting suspiciously in the building. He was found in the ladies toilets would you believe' she explained. This confirmed any doubt in my mind about turning down the job, they clearly didn't know it was me and I couldn't run the risk, however great, of them finding out further down the line.

'Yes he sounds very strange indeed, maybe he was having a hard time of things too' I suggested.

'By all accounts he was a strawberry short of a fruit basket' she replied.

It was the night of the dinner party, the house was alive with activity as the four of us chopped, blended and blitzed a variety of ingredients into submission. As usual despite spending half the day preparing the food it had suddenly crept towards the hour of arrival and the doorbell sounded just as I was holding the chicken with an industrial pair of oven gloves. Irene immediately made for the front door to my horror and I quickly asked Rachel to intercept. Barry was at the door, immaculately turned out and brandishing a bottle of vintage red wine.

'Are you Colin from the dating site?' asked Irene.

'Er...no I'm Barry a friend of Tim's' he replied nervously.

'Wait until I get you upstairs' she exclaimed, winking at him. He clearly felt very uncomfortable at the thought of this, I couldn't imagine why!

'Hello Barry, please excuse Irene. She came with the house' I joked.

'Ah right, I can give you the number of a good exorcist' he quipped. Rachel shot me a disconcerted glance.

'If you'd like to take a seat in there I will bring you a beer to get you started' I suggested pointing in the direction of the front room.

'Is this the waiting room?' he replied as he strode instead into the kitchen. Clearly my attempts to keep him out of the area had fallen on deaf ears. Why did people insist on talking to you relentlessly when you were trying to prepare food? There was presumably a giant human magnet in the kitchen that only activated during dinner parties.

'Rachel I think Irene will be better off in her room. All this excitement will be too much, you know how she gets' I stated as if I was someone who was respected in their own house.

'I'm not missing this for the world' Irene interjected.

'Irene this is a dinner for my friends and I. It's a chance to catch up with people I haven't seen for a while. I would like everyone to please allow me some time alone with them' I reasoned.

'Very well Weaselface' she replied before turning away and heading towards the stairs.

'Sorry, did she just call you Weaselface?' That's brilliant!' said Barry, chuckling away to himself. I'd never been called Weaselface in my life and to the best of my knowledge didn't even remotely resemble one. In fact I couldn't look less like a weasel if I tried.

'She says such nice things to me' I offered, having now completely lost my train of thought with the cooking. The door rang again.

'I'll get it' offered Barry. I hoped they would now de-camp to the dining room to allow me to finish the food. But no, in came Barry and Terry to resume the food interruption process.

'Alright Weaselface' said Terry.

'You told him?' I said to Barry.

'No that was our nickname for you in the office' replied Terry. Both he and Barry were smiling like two schoolboys playing a prank. At least I hoped it was a prank, either way I had a feeling that I was stuck with the name forever.

The food and wine flowed as the evening went on. It was great to see the guys again although the infamous Mad Dog failed to put in an appearance. Perhaps he felt guilty about the way things had ended. Then again perhaps he didn't, I would never really know.

'Pass the wine Terry' ordered Barry, who was starting to become worse for wear.

'You're not driving I hope' I enquired.

'I don't drink and drive. But that doesn't stop me drinking before I drive' quipped Barry.

'So if you had to choose between Irene or Maureen from accounts which one would you go for?' asked Barry.

'Oh that's terrible...I would have to go for Maureen as she at least is compos mentis' replied Terry. 'What about that new girl or the cleaner' replied Terry in retaliatory fashion.

'Christ they are both the work of Satan when it comes to the looks department' said Barry.

'Hang on did you say new girl?' I enquired after nearly choking on a piece of satay chicken.

'Yes we have a new girl that started with us last week, she is helping out with the admin and account management calls. We've been getting further and further behind since you left'.

'So you've hired someone for half the price to replace me?'

'Well not directly' Terry replied, sensing I was a little perturbed by this revelation.

'I know someone who could've helped you out' I said.

'Who?' asked Barry.

'That's not even funny Baz, if anything else comes up can one of you let me know?'

'Sure we'll put in a good word for you' he responded. Put in a good word? I couldn't believe what I was hearing.

'Well I would appreciate it, there really isn't much out there at the minute'

'Will do Captain' said Terry. I realised at that moment that any thoughts of them rushing to pick up the phone at the first opportunity was misguided. I couldn't believe they hadn't even considered calling me when a vacancy had arisen. They were working on the assumption I would contact them.

'Changing the subject slightly, a mate of mine works in town. Some guy turned up at their office pretending he worked there and was caught red handed putting up a webcam in the ladies toilet'

'I was not putting it up-'I barked before my brain had a chance to intercept my mouth and disengage.

They sat in stunned silence.

After the guys had gone I poured myself one last whisky and sat alone in the lounge. It was disappointing they hadn't even thought to ask me about the vacancy at work. Furthermore I found they were talking about new customers and staff members I didn't know and I felt even more isolated from the company. The world had moved on without me and I had been replaced by a student who had no experience of life, the universe or Paradox. Listening to them talking at times it felt like I wasn't even there, a bit like a time traveller who was viewing a conversation but wasn't visible to the other parties. I would gladly partake in some time travel now. Glancing at my phone I saw missed calls from Richard Long and another from David at the hospital. He was no doubt wondering how the drug trial was coming along. I would have to contact him in due course but there were bigger fish to fry first.

A Friend in Need

After the dinner party I felt even more confused and lost than I had before, if that was possible. It had been great to see the guys again but I felt very detached from the corporate world and it left me to ponder whether I even wanted to be in such an environment any more. But it was all I knew - at my age was it really possible to re-train as something entirely different? I had quite fancied being an architect when I left school and then after realising that further education wasn't exactly a walk in the park I opted to try my hand at working instead. The lure of cold hard cash and the discovery of alcohol and women ensured I never returned to education. One of those was true at least.

In the days that followed I sat solidly in front of the computer and applied for a plethora of jobs in the faint hope of at least securing one interview. I read online that a lot of agencies were simply canvassing for jobs that didn't actually exist in order to load their portfolio with potential recruits should the right vacancy arise. I felt this was very unfair, especially as people like me were spending hours applying for these roles with no real idea of their authenticity. It was a cruel practice if it was true, but what choice did the unemployed have? Every route seemed to lead back to the internet. Over the course of those days my phone buzzed constantly and every time I looked excitedly at the screen the anticipation turned to dismay. The majority of calls were from Richard Long, the hospital chasing the results of the trials, the roofer chasing payment and various other companies wanting me to spend money I didn't have on things I didn't need. The anxiety was starting to increase and the tablets I had been given were sat in my drawer gathering dust. Money was starting to become very tight and I was now reliant on the credit card, which was steadily increasing in terms of the amount owed. The problem with this strategy was the lack of incoming money to be able to repay the debt, time was starting to become of the essence now. On top of feeling generally lost and bewildered, the general lack of support from Rachel was disconcerting and I was beginning to question whether things were as rosy as I once thought. I couldn't be sure if these thoughts were the result of an altered perspective or if they were realities I had never dared to face historically. Sometimes it seemed you could muddle through life oblivious to certain facets being unsuitable as long as nothing terrible happened that exposed the frailties hidden beneath the façade. This I feared was the case and the thought struck me that it was only the constant spending and lifestyle that was papering over the cavernous cracks. I wondered if Rachel felt the same after all these years. That was another issue, we had a communication problem. Friends of mine had told me as much when we first got together but I was blinded by something I believed to be love at the time. It was a long time since I recalled how that felt but oddly I hadn't consciously thought about it for many years. Not since I had last 'dealt' with feelings for Caitlin and accepted there was too much to risk losing in making a play for someone who may not even be interested in me in a romantic capacity. Over time that desire had eased and I told myself that it was for the best. The longer I went without seeing her, the easier it became to justify it to myself. To a certain extent I believed that but if I was brutally honest it was a case of holding back a metaphorical field of wild horses. The equine beasts were on the edge of restraint now that our friendship had been rekindled and this was adding to the sense of chaos that had besieged me in recent times. All things considered the world as I knew it had been turned

132

upside down and in many ways it felt like we were on a rollercoaster ride with no track. I really had no idea how things were going to turn out and what state we would be in at the end of it all. The redundancy had made me feel very isolated and now I was questioning everything that I used to take for granted. My confidence was plummeting like a large lump of granite into a deep ravine and my judgement was becoming more clouded by the day. People had told me that being made redundant was second only to bereavement in terms of stress and at the time I had been dismissive, my brash confidence bordering on arrogance. But the reality was that it left me with feelings of rejection and despair. Before this I knew exactly who I was and where I was going in life. I loved my job and felt respected. I was proud of everything we had built together and never (Caitlin aside) really questioned the purpose of it all. If I became ill I had medical insurance to take care of it, if I needed help with stress or legal matters I could call our employee helpline who were there round the clock to provide support. I never used these things and ironically the only time I could do with such help was the present day, after the redundancy! Not only that, I had lost my car and found myself enduring the delights of mingling with the general public having become reliant on the bus and train. It was all a foreign experience to me and heightened my sense of being out on a limb. A man is a sum of his parts and when most of them are taken away it leaves you with very little to work with.

Every day I saw people going about their business, commuting to work and blissfully unaware of how lucky they were to still have a job as the county collapsed around their ears. I so longed to be one of those people again, to have a purpose other than keeping Irene from burning the house down or walking around with her undesirables on show. Not only did I lose my job and all of the perks, one of the hardest parts was losing your identity and friends. Without warning people I had seen every day for twenty years were suddenly removed from my life. I couldn't just walk into another room

133

and engage in cheeky banter with the irrepressible Dawn from Accounts. Or wind up Barry by unplugging his phone earpiece then calling his number and watching as he picked it up and realised he had been duped. I felt a terrible sense of loss and nothing seemed to make up for that. Being a man meant that you were expected to simply pull yourself together and get on with things, but as much as I tried it felt like I was falling apart at the seams. The anxiety wasn't exactly helping the situation - having never had to deal with such an emotion it was having a profound effect on me. I was actually subconsciously developing a fear of anxiety itself, which of course was a self perpetuating cycle. I didn't really know what I was anxious about half of the time. The recession was ubiquitous by nature and everywhere I looked there was more damning evidence of its existence and effect on society. The so-called 'credit crunch' was basically an excuse for lenders to call in their debts and protect their shareholder's arses regardless of how it impacted on the general public. These financial institutions had given far too much away and now the tide had turned were demanding it all back without any acknowledgement of their role in the process. It made me sick to my stomach, I was lucky as I had the means to pay off the debt but others would be in serious trouble - as would I if I didn't find a way of repaying my mounting credit card debt. The increasing amount of boarded up properties in the local area said it all - people and businesses were sinking fast. I found myself looking around the house and feeling like I didn't deserve any of it any more, that I was a failure and it was a bitter pill to swallow. I was angry with my employer for casting me onto the veritable scrapheap at the height of the recession and even more annoyed with the credit card company for putting the knife in at the same time. This was my biggest test of character to date. Add to that the various problems with the house requiring expenditure and Irene's decreasing mental health it was a cauldron as foul as a bucket of sparrows.

The nights were drawing in as autumn began. Greens became browns and leaves made their silent ascension to the ground where they would rest until they faded away. It was rather symbolic of my own existence at this moment in time. After dinner I received a call from David who had resorted to using a number previously unrecognised by my phone - in the faint hope it was a prospective employer I answered it.

'Tim, thank god you're alive I was worried the drugs had finished you off'

'Ah sorry Dave, I've been a bit pre-occupied'

'Have you tried them? I need to record your results buddy'

'I keep meaning to and the truth is I really could use them'

'If you're worried about it we can discuss it over a pint later?'

'I'm sure it's fine. I don't suppose you have any actual jobs at work?'

'Nothing buddy, I'm afraid they froze recruitment, austerity and all that'

'A familiar story' I replied dejectedly.

'See you down the Hare and Hounds then' he replied before terminating the call without even saying goodbye, just like they did on films. I never had the nerve to just disconnect without signalling my intention to do so. It didn't seem very British.

Rachel had some friends over for a 'girlie' evening. I decided against going to the pub and instead opted to retire to bed early as it had been a long few days of constant internet job applications. Irene had performed her usual trick of presenting me with some envelopes that she had been storing for some time. I was now dreading the post in case it was a demand for more money from somebody. It felt like there was a conspiracy at work at times. I stripped off ready for bed and in my full naked glory perched upon the toilet and proceeded to open the latest postal offerings. Some people read magazines on the toilet, I preferred to read letters. To my horror one of the letters was from a firm I had prospected offering me an interview for the previous Wednesday. I was absolutely livid and the futility of venting this annoyance towards Irene made it all the more frustrating. Even if I ordered her to keep away from the post she would forget about it as soon as she regressed back to the 1960's again. My only hope was that the job was still unfilled and then maybe I could blame the postal system. I didn't realise companies still communicated by letter in this modern age. I opened the next envelope and fully expected it to be irrelevant compared to the first one. How wrong I was – I stared at the letter in a state of abject shock that was beyond anything I had known for some time. The bastard credit card company had slashed my limit following a 'review' and it was barely more than the amount I now owed on the card. It was absolutely beyond comprehension that they could do this – not content with taking my redundancy pay they were now minimising their risk further by cutting my only access to money. How the actual fuck was I going to pay the mortgage in a few weeks time? This was in real terms a disaster of gargantuan proportions and my heart was thumping like a drum skin belonging to a heavy metal band. It was all my rib cage could do to prevent it bursting free. I was having a full on panic attack, my breathing had become restricted and I found myself gasping for air. It was truly terrifying and in the recesses of my brain I recalled you should breathe into a paper bag to restore parity. It struck me they didn't specify what sized paper bag but there wasn't time to research this. Luckily I found a paper bag with some books in and tipped everything onto the bed and frantically began inhaling and exhaling into the bag. I was feeling light headed and very distraught which was making it harder to breathe sensibly. The bag was not helping and I then realised it had a large tear where one of the book corners had punctured it. I threw the bag on the bed and lurched downstairs, my only focus was finding another paper bag and quickly as my head spun and my heart pounded. I was petrified as this had never happened before and I couldn't calm myself down sufficiently to reduce the symptoms. I reached the hall and looked frantically round in cartoon fashion before dashing to the kitchen where I desperately threw open drawers and cupboards, rifling through the contents manically whilst making strange breathing noises akin to someone choking. Finally I found a small paper bag with candles in, I them over the floor and sunk to my knees and wheezed into the bag whilst making the unusual high pitched noises. Eventually I felt my breathing return to some sense of normality and it was as if someone had unclamped my lungs. I felt drained and slowly opened my eyes. As the room came into focus it became apparent Rachel and her friends were perched around the kitchen island and were staring in horror as I sat there naked on the floor.

After the panic attack I paced around the bedroom trying to think logically and work out the next move without inducing another episode. I knew if I called them they would say they reserved the right to change the limits whenever it suited them, just like they reserved the right to mess around with the interest rates. It felt like they were on a mission to financially destroy me. I decided I wanted to have it out with them regardless. I called them on the landline and then made countless option choices before being put into a queue for an eternity.

'Good evening is that Tim Fellows?' asked a man of Scottish descent.

'Yes it is' I confirmed.

'Could I just take your date of birth?'

'You mean the same date of birth I just entered? It's 24th February 1978' I replied sarcastically.

'We do need to-'

'Yes I'm fully aware you need me to repeat information whilst calling this premium rate number' I snapped.

'I'm sorry you feel like that Mr Fellows. How can I help

137

you this evening?'

'Well I hope you can. After paying off my entire balance with my redundancy money I have just received a letter advising me you've slashed my limit to £400'.

'Let me just have a look for you Mr Fellows'. I could hear furious tapping. In the background I could also hear another conversation – an advisor telling another customer they had reviewed their limit as per the terms and conditions. So I was clearly not the only one.

'Right, it looks as if there has been a review of your account and the lending team have set a lower limit for you' he finally explained.

'Okay, that bit I already knew – my question is why? Have I ever missed a payment? My credit rating is excellent, so why have you reduced my limit?'

'Yes I can see you have run your account very well and no Sir, there are no late payments. I will speak to lending and come back to you' he replied promisingly.

'Okay thanks'. I listened to three tracks of music, including the theme to the X-Files which seemed appropriate in the circumstances. The line crackled and he was back.

'Hello Mr Fellows, I've spoken to lending and they explained that if you look at clause F21 you will see we reserve the right to review your limit at any time'.

'Right, we've established this already – can they perform another review and increase it given my excellent payment history?' I asked in an exasperated tone. My heart was starting to beat faster again.

'I did ask about that. They said you would be okay for a slight increase as long as there were no signs of using the card to pay for utilities as that would indicate financial distress'

'Well I have had to pay the council tax using the card' I explained.

'Yes that is what they told me and I'm afraid that counts against you' he advised coldly.

'What the fuck has it got to do with them what I spend

my money on?' I ranted.

'We have to be very careful in light of the recession - there are new rules around lending responsibly'

'It's a pity these rules weren't in place when I took the card out. Bloody ridiculous!' I slammed the phone down and sat on the bed with my head in my hands. I couldn't believe the ludicrous rules they were abiding by to protect themselves at all costs. I couldn't sleep now and it was only 8pm so I decided to get dressed and leave the house for a bit of fresh air to clear my head. I strode down the stairs and there was Irene waiting to ascend at the bottom.

'Thank you for not passing me the post I've missed an interview now' I snapped.

'If you don't get a job soon you will have to move out. I can't have any freeloaders living here' she replied before heading upstairs with her dress tucked into her underwear at the back.

'Gladly' I replied before leaving, remembering to slam the front door.

After disgracing myself in front of Rachel's friends and taking in the latest bombshell I walked aimlessly around the leafy streets of suburbia. Perhaps I was hoping the answer to my problems would come to me in some sort of epiphany. At the very least I was hopeful of an alien abduction to take me away from this situation although I would politely decline the probe option. The evening air had a slight chill that was hinting of colder times ahead and the majority of my neighbourhood were camped in front of their televisions in anticipation of the evenings viewing. I couldn't recall the last time I had enjoyed a relaxing night in the front room - it must've been a while before the redundancy. I realised the magnitude of the situation with finances meant I had little choice but to gain employment in any capacity regardless of the type of industry or role. The option of being choosy had been taken away. I could complain to the credit card company but that would take thirty days for a response and what would the basis of my complaint be? It wasn't their fault I had organised my finances in such a manner. It hadn't occurred to me they might reduce the credit limit and that oversight had now put me to the sword. The real problem was that I now had no way of meeting the next mortgage payment and the chances were that we would lose our house. There was nobody I could ask to borrow it from, my parents were scraping by on the state pension and Rachel's only surviving parent was Irene.

Deep in my thoughts I had not taken any notice of my whereabouts and found myself approaching the Hare and Hounds public house. I could make out the impressionist style human shapes conversing over pints of beer through the opaque glass windows. Smoke rose from the chimney into the night sky indicating either a welcoming real fireplace or a chef with timing issues. I recalled David had invited me for a drink and given the events of this evening thought I would take him up on it. I opened the main door and was greeted by a busy and convivial bar area, the locals were out in force enjoying a noisy pint and chewing the fat of life.

'Tim!' came a voice from somewhere in the throng. It was David - he squeezed past a group of men who were adding to the general congestion around the bar.

'Hello Dave, sorry I'm late it's been a bit of an evening' I explained, as if I had intended to join him all along.

'No worries fellow – sorry no pun intended' he replied.

'Ha! Listen there's something I really need to speak to you about' I said.

'Sure thing, as it happens I really need your advice on something too'

'My advice? You must be desperate' I quipped.

'That girl I told you I like – she's here tonight!' he exclaimed.

'Look, I'll be honest I don't even understand the woman I've been married to for years, but I'll try and help'

'She's over there but I'm not that confident with matters of the heart'

'Based on your day job I would beg to differ'

'I spend so much time trying to regulate hearts that I don't know how to make them race. Can you go and speak to her and mention you have a friend who is rich, charming and charismatic. I will then appear and hey presto. Just get me an intro please'.

'Won't she wonder where this other man is that I've described?' I joked.

'Nice one. Come on Tim you know I'd do it for you'

'Where is she?'

'She's round the other side of the bar sat by the fireplace in the mauve top. Short spikey brown hair'

'For Christ's sake.....alright then but in return I would like unlimited alcohol to drown my sorrows'

'It's a deal, it's a steal....'

'It's someone else's quote...'

'I knew you wouldn't let me down. I'll bring the drinks round buddy'

I worked my way around the bar, weaving artfully through the myriad of people whilst carefully observing the unwritten rule of not knocking fellow males pints over the floor. As the fireplace came into view I noticed the intended target with the mauve top, she was talking animatedly to a group of friends. Then I experienced the third horror of the night - the lady in the mauve top was Caitlin. I froze on the spot then ducked behind a group of men. How on earth could I be party to setting her up with someone else? My tired mind raced yet again, this was a disaster. Was it morally fair of me to jeopardise either of their future happiness when I was in no position to even contemplate anything with her myself - even if she did happen to feel the same? I had to accept she could meet someone at any time and it really wasn't any of my business. Having said that I would prefer not to play Cupid where she was concerned. But what choice was there? I had to at least speak to her even just because I wanted to regardless of the motive. I made my way over.

'Oh my god – Tim!' she shrieked as she saw me approach.

She halted her conversation and came running over with outstretched arms and gave me a big hug. In that moment it felt like all of my troubles had just evaporated and I wanted to stay wrapped in her arms indefinitely. She was wearing eye liner and this really enhanced the hypnotic blue of her eyes.

'How are you?' I asked.

'I'm great thanks – everyone this is Tim. The guy I was telling you about' she announced, giving me a look. Telling them what I wondered? Her three friends stood up and shook my hand whilst introducing themselves with names I knew I'd forget instantly.

'So what are you doing here? I thought you never went out' she asked.

'Well I've had a bit of an evening if I'm honest'

'Aww I'm just going outside for some fresh air it's a bit hot in here. You can tell me all about it' she said with the greatest amount of sincerity I had encountered for some time. I followed her back out into the evening air. We stood near the smokers, who were banished from the pub for their desire to destroy their lungs and others around them. I recounted the tale of the night's events and she sympathised – it almost felt like a counselling session. Whilst I felt bad unloading all of my troubles on her it was very cathartic.

'So now you've listened to all of my problems what about yours? It's the least I can do' I offered.

'Oh you know - life is fairly shit. I'm just muddling along but I'm not getting any younger and it seems I'm invisible to the male population'. Not to me I wanted to say, but couldn't. She looked amazing as ever and gazing into her eyes was like nothing I'd encountered with anyone else but her.

'Are you seriously telling me there's nobody, it's a travesty!' was all I could say.

'That's very kind of you to say Tim, I wish the rest of the men felt the same' she said, hugging me tightly. I planted a kiss on her head and we hugged for a minute under the gaze of the moon. Apparently under the gaze of another – David was now standing there looking at me in complete astonishment as we were entwined in each others arms.

'Thanks a bunch' he uttered before turning and storming off into the night. I realised how it looked and also at that moment how I'd completely forgotten I was supposed to be trying to set him up with Caitlin. The time had flashed past and he had obviously been wondering where we'd gone.

'Sorry – what was that?' asked Caitlin.

'Oh don't worry about him' I replied without actually explaining anything. Nothing else mattered at that moment in time. I hadn't seen him for years and to be quite frank I could wait another twenty.

'He was freaking me out staring across the bar at me' she said.

'Yes he does that sometimes'.

After walking Caitlin home I made my way back to the house, my head was filled with all manner of confusion, everything was reaching fever pitch and the path ahead was very uncertain. I entered the house and it was in darkness downstairs so I fetched a drink of water from the kitchen before attempting to quietly creep up the stairs, which was going well until I dropped my phone halfway up. It banged against the stair rail as it bounced downwards and clattered on the laminated flooring in the hall below. After retrieving the phone and hurriedly re-constructing it I then headed back upstairs to the bedroom. The gentle glow of the bedside lamps illuminated the landing, it was nearly midnight. Walking into the bedroom Rachel was sat at her dressing table, she had her frosty face on. By frosty I meant her normal face.

'Where have you been?' she demanded to know.

'I went for a walk then met Dave at the pub' I replied half truthfully.

'I've never trusted you' she snarled.

'Rachel what's wrong? Are you going to tell me or am I supposed to guess what's going on?'

She then stood up and started waving her arms in my general direction.

'It's you, you, you!' she exclaimed.

'Yes you have correctly identified me' I quipped, trying to lighten the mood.

'I can't talk to you because you make jokes out of everything, I never have been able to' she started to explain.

'I don't mean to, it's just my way'

'You need to pull yourself together Tim – be a man. All this sitting around feeling sorry for yourself is no good'

'I'm not sitting around-'

'I don't see you tearing up the streets, your behaviour is becoming increasingly erratic and another thing – you've let yourself go. Look at you' she stated whilst glancing up and down me with a look of disgust. She might as well have plunged a machete into me.

'Have you any fucking idea what it's like? In fact what the real world is like? I'm sick of supporting a house full of freeloaders. Why don't you go and get a job and I'll sit around all day finding a variety of things to complain about' I snapped without even thinking. There was a moment of silence whilst both parties paused to digest everything. Had I gone too far? I wasn't even sure if I cared.

'You're hopeless' she remarked. With that she stormed out of the room and a few seconds later out of the house. I sat on the bed shaking with anger and I could feel the blood racing around my veins as if furiously seeking an outlet. I half expected it to start spraying out of my ears at any moment. Her attitude was unbelievable and after all these years of providing a more than comfortable lifestyle the knives had come out and were glistening from the recent thrust into the remaining strands of my confidence. I waited for the sound as it plummeted into the abyss and hit the bottom but there was nothing. I had to find a way of proving to everyone that I hadn't suddenly become a failure and maybe the person I needed to convince the most was me. I became aware of footsteps at the bedroom door.

144

'Daddy I can't sleep with all the shouting' said Ellen.

'I'm sorry honey there will be no more tonight' I replied apologetically.

'Why is Mummy nice to everyone but us?' she asked.

'She doesn't mean it' I tried to explain, but it didn't seem fair to expand on the machinations of Rachel's complex brain to a young child. I barely understood her myself.

'Can we read a book together?' she enquired, using the fluttering eyelashes to great effect.

'Sure thing cheekbones' I conceded. It would be great to be lost for a while in the world of children's books where everything had a happy ending.

'This letter came for you' she announced, handing me a crumpled envelope. I looked wearily at it before sliding a finger along the opening to open it and see what manner of filth was lurking inside. To my absolute surprise it was headed 'Job Application- Sales Executive' and was inviting me for an interview in two days time. The letter went on to provide details of the role and the assessment that I would undergo. Then I noticed the interview address was at their head office in Scotland of all places. I had no choice – it was time for Tim Fellows to rise like a phoenix from the burning embers of his tattered life and save the day.

Sense and Senility

I woke up on the bed still wearing my clothes from the night before, I must have fallen asleep unexpectedly although had no recollection. As the morning came into focus and the haze of the preceding slumber lifted a few items brought themselves to my attention. Firstly, I had to find a way of getting to Stirling in forty eight hours and secondly I needed to make peace with Rachel. Neither task seemed particularly easy given the lack of available finances and lack of available wife. I presumed she had gone to unload her perceived traumas on one of her friends, who would no doubt provide confirmation that everything she thought was actually true. Whenever she thought she had been wronged her friends would provide the necessary verification in order to vindicate her indulgent narcissism. What were friends for? I was fairly certain they wouldn't be advising her to rush straight home and sort everything out as there was no sport in it for their entertainment. I sent her a text asking if she was okay and informed her of the interview. Hopefully this news would make her realise that I was making progress and that everything would be okay – the Fellows ship would be stabilised and we could all get on with our lives again. Whilst waiting for her reply I looked at flights on the internet - they were all ridiculously expensive and in excess of the money available to me. Again I found myself cursing the credit card company for their actions and the timing of them more so. Yet again it was almost as if they were conspiring to stuff things up for me.

The clock seemed to be ticking faster than ever and every minute that passed represented time lost in the quest to get to the interview. Rachel had not replied so I tried to call her mobile – straight to voicemail. She was playing the ignoring game. Her sulks were legendary and generally lasted for up to three days. It was on the other hand useful if I wanted some peace and quiet – all I had to do was annoy her which wasn't exactly difficult. I could hear Irene and Ellen moving around the house and wondered what on earth I would do with them if Rachel didn't return. Spurred on by this panic driven thought I proceeded to call Rachel again and then started the arduous task of calling her friends. The downside to this was they would all be aware of the argument and would then make contact with her to obtain the gory details and put their views across. All of this would achieve the ultimate end result of slowing down the fairly vital bit – making contact with me. I knew some of her friends were lying, they clearly knew something had happened and were only embarrassing themselves by pretending otherwise. I made a mental note to return the favour if their husbands ever came to stay at ours following a disagreement. Not that such a thing ever occurred as most of them had been ground down over the years to such an extent they didn't waste their energy on arguments. I realised there was a sense of irony in that thought. It was typical that the one time I really needed Rachel to be at home she was off the radar. I found her stubbornness incredibly frustrating and on this occasion it was only serving to accentuate the feelings of discontentment I was having about the marriage. Why did she have to be so difficult? I tried to look at things from her perspective and I appreciated that in hindsight my behaviour had probably seemed a little erratic as she so eloquently phrased it. She wouldn't understand if I even tried to explain the whirlwind of feelings that were churning around my brain leaving everything in tatters. I longed for the assured permanent job and all of the comforts that came with it. My chest pounded, my heart ached, everything I had known had been taken away and my confidence had all but deserted me. Nothing seemed certain any more. Everywhere I looked I observed the effects of the recession. Building developments left abandoned, hordes of unemployed at the agencies, it was in the media twenty four hours a day – there was no escape. But thinking about it was not going to help me travel to Scotland. I needed a hard and fast plan. So hard and fast you could set a fence post in it. Another option was the train. Subsequent research on the internet revealed this was equally as expensive as flying. To think that the government were trying to encourage people to use public transport – it was so prohibitively priced. Did they not realise that by lowering the price more people might use it?

The time was now half past ten and there was still no plan or Rachel to speak of. Furthermore I couldn't think of anyone that could look after Irene or even be willing to do so. This was a disaster of sizeable proportions. With the onset of panic and a degree of chest pain I rang Rachel again, this time leaving a terse message on her voicemail that included the words awkward, selfish and idiot. Ellen appeared at the bedroom door.

'Daddy I think someone is trying to call Mummy's mobile' she announced, holding Rachel's mobile in her outstretched hand.

'Ah...that explains the lack of response' I replied, then realised she would return to a barrage of missed calls and an abusive voicemail message.

'When is Mummy coming home?'

'I don't know Ellen, she has gone to stay with her friend for a little while' I lied.

'Which one?'

'She said something about one of her friends from yoga'

'Maybe they can do yoga together and she will feel better' she replied. It was all so simple in the mind of a child.

'Yes I hope so' I replied.

By the time I had showered and gotten dressed it was

midday and there was still no sign of Rachel. In desperation I tried calling a couple of friends to offer them the opportunity of house sitting but as soon as they realised Irene was part of the package they politely declined. As I sat on the bed the grim realisation took hold – I had no choice other than to take Irene and Ellen to Scotland with me! It was possibly the least desirable outcome that I could have imagined but these were desperate times and this opportunity was too good to pass up. My only hope was that Rachel's car was outside. I glanced out of the bay window and to my absolute relief it was glistening in the sun on the asphalt driveway. I reasoned that she had left me no choice with her disappearing act and this in turn justified my decision to borrow it. If we left today I would have enough money left on the credit card to cover the petrol and pay for a cheap bed and breakfast. The thought of spending the next day and half on the road with Irene filled me with terror beyond belief. But what other choice did I have? I marched downstairs to relay this news to the un-expecting duo.

'Ladies can I have your attention please' I demanded.

'You can't just walk in here like this, Tim will be furious' replied Irene.

'I am Tim' I replied exasperatedly whilst looking up to the heavens for assistance.

'He will be back soon, then you'll-'

'Look I haven't got time for this trip down Amnesia Avenue. The long and short of it is this – I need to get to Scotland for an interview and there is nobody that can look after you two. Therefore we are all going in the car unless anyone has a better idea?' I asked rhetorically.

'Do they have Scottish people up there?' enquired Irene.

'I think there may be the odd one or two' was all I could furnish that nonsensical question with.

'Yippee I've always wanted to go to Scotland – where is it?' asked an excited Ellen.

'Only several hundred miles north of here - now we need to get going quickly. Ellen can you get some of your clothes ready and then we'll help you pack too Irene'.

'I am packed ready to go' she replied.

'You can't be – I've only just told you about it'

'I've been living out of a suitcase for weeks. I'm not putting my clothes in the wardrobe – this hotel is a dump' she scalded before turning around and trotting off upstairs. I couldn't recall the last time she said anything that vaguely resembled reality. Surely there had to be an easier option than taking her with us.

After some frantic packing and last minute security checks around the house we left a note for Rachel and boarded her Polo.

'It's been years since I last went to the sea, I'm looking forward to this' said Irene.

'Yes we'll be at the sea soon enough' I humoured her. If she wasn't careful we would take a detour to the sea and I could then throw her in it. I decided to keep that thought to myself.

A quick inspection of the dashboard revealed the information I was dreading –the car was bereft of diesel. This was rather annoying as I only had limited funds to play with. No wonder Rachel walked to her unknown destination last night! Part of me was worried something sinister had happened to her and I contemplated reporting her as missing. But the police don't take missing adults seriously unless they've been gone for some time. We drove to the nearest garage and I treated the diesel tank to a fresh intake of fuel. The tank glugged away contentedly as it gorged on a large chunk of the remaining vestiges of my credit card limit. A couple of tanks should cover it I thought to myself.

'Daddy the seat is wet in the back' announced Ellen, poking her head out of the rear window.

'Maybe the sun roof is leaking or something, it has been raining' I suggested.

'It doesn't smell like rain' she replied and then turned to look at Irene. I realised what this meant - Irene's incontinence had struck again. This was going to be the longest trip of my entire life and we were only a few miles into it. Luckily there was a shop in the village that sold a variety of clothes for the elderly at rock bottom prices – I made a note to stop at the Charity Shop en route and buy a replacement floral garment. Not to mention new underwear and some incontinence pads from the supermarket.

We arrived at the said charity shop and managed to find a space outside. Upon entering I noticed the familiar musty aroma that befitted such establishments. It was synonymous with all charity shops the length and breadth of England. I made my way to the counter.

'Are you taking donations?' I asked the young lady.

'Yes what sort of donation? We can't take electrical items at this shop' she advised.

'Oh it's nothing electrical – just this lady here' I joked pointing to Irene. The counter girl laughed nervously, she was unsure if I was joking. So was I for that matter.

'Have you got a bucket and spade' Irene asked the lady.

'Erm...no we don't tend to sell them in here' she replied.

'Well you might want to think about it, given you're by the sea – you're missing a trick' Irene countered. I motioned to the girl that Irene was a lunatic by way of a shaking head and eyes rolling up to the heavens. Then looked back to discover Irene had seen me. The tiniest flicker of guilt crept across my conscience at that moment. It didn't linger for long. I turned away and started gathering dresses that I thought Irene would like to wear while Ellen was busy looking at the children's books and toys. After collating a bundle of chintz dresses with all manner of floral pattern I turned around to discover Irene had disappeared.

'Where did she go?' I asked the girl at the counter.

'In there' she pointed towards the changing room. She must have seen something she liked and was trying it on. I was pleased to finally receive a small modicum of co-operation from her. This momentary joy was short lived however when her wizened hand drew back the curtain to reveal her clothing choice.

'Irene that's a wedding dress – what are you doing?'

'I might meet someone at Gretna Green'

'There are two flaws with your plan. The first is we're not going to Gretna Green. The second and most fundamental flaw is you are unlikely to meet a man who is hanging around the place in his wedding attire on the off chance a suitable spinster appears out of the blue on that very day'.

'Some chance is better than no chance'.

'Look, I'm not arguing we haven't got the time for this. Can you take the dress off please?'

'You can't make me' she replied with all the stubbornness of her daughter. I contemplated the options available to me.

After leaving the charity shop thirty pounds lighter we decanted the purchases into our suitcases and used the carrier bags to line the back seat. So at least the wedding dress she was now wearing would not become soaked. I couldn't believe she had put me on the spot like that – but I could hardly start wrestling the dress off of her in front of the shop assistant and other customers. I felt bad for Ellen as she had behaved perfectly and asked for nothing, whereas Irene had acted like a spoilt child and had a small fortune spent on her. I started the car and we then embarked on the first leg of the journey, which was to escape the smaller roads of suburbia and make our way towards the motorway. After a short time Irene announced she needed the toilet again. At least she had the presence of mind to inform me in advance this time. Maybe the wedding dress wasn't such a bad thing – she might actually want to keep it urine free for her fictitious big day. I could use this notion to my advantage.

'We'll stop at the supermarket Irene it's just here. Thank you for telling me this time, you wouldn't want to ruin that lovely wedding dress' I suggested. She was gazing distantly out of the window so whether or not anything I had just said had registered in her addled brain was debatable.

We entered the supermarket and received the kind of look you would expect when accompanied by a geriatric in a wedding dress. If people in the local area didn't already think I was insane they certainly would do now. I just hoped Caitlin wasn't in the vicinity. For once however I hoped Rachel was. Irene relieved her troubled bladder in the supermarket toilet while Ellen and I waited outside near the checkouts. Eventually she emerged in her wedding attire.

'All okay?' I enquired.

'Yes thank you I'd forgotten how difficult it is go to toilet in a wedding dress' she remarked.

'Oh crikey yes – you need four hands' I conceded having given it no thought whatsoever beforehand.

'It's okay a nice gentleman helped hold it up for me, keep it off the floor'

'Gentleman? You didn't go in the......you did didn't you' I hadn't thought to check which toilet she'd gone into. She looked at me as if I was the mad one.

'Come on fuckface lets go' she ordered in her own inimitable style.

'Charming. We need to get some provisions for the journey – can you go and get some juice and I'll grab some sandwiches to eat on the way' I asked in a rare authoritative tone. She wandered off towards the drinks aisle while Ellen and I made our way to the refrigerator bearing freshly made sandwiches. We made our selections and chose a bacon, lettuce and tomato roll for Irene then weaved in and out of the other shoppers to buy some fruit. After selecting our fruit of choice I turned around and Irene had re-appeared empty handed, but was flanked by two men of Jewish persuasion complete with skull caps and long ringlets of black hair.

'Irene – I said JUICE!' I exclaimed. How embarrassing was this?

'I'm sorry he gets a bit confused' she turned to the Jewish men and raised her eyes to the heavens. One of the men reached out and went to shake my hand. I quickly moved the bacon roll to the other hand in order to reciprocate.

'My name is Aaron' he announced. I returned the gesture.

'I am Tim, otherwise known as Fuckface'.

Finally after the supermarket and charity shop ordeals we climbed aboard the Polo and resumed our journey. I felt confident that we had everything we needed now and surely nothing else could hinder our progress apart from the obvious traffic on the motorway and Irene's temperamental bladder.

Ticket to Ride

There had been moments in my life when I'd felt like everything was against me and this was one of them. As we sat by the roadside next to Rachel's stricken Polo I mused that even her car had emulated her lack of support in my hour of need. It had never let her down in years of ownership and pointless trips to nail bars but the one time I needed it for something important it suffered a catastrophic engine failure. Of course in an attempt to cut back on our outgoings I had cancelled luxuries such as breakdown cover and had no means to re-instate it. The clock was ticking and a large portion of my remaining wealth resided in the fuel tank of the wretched vehicle. The three of us sat by the roadside and watched a multitude of fully functioning cars soar past as my hopes of reaching Stirling faded quicker than an X-Factor winner's career.

'This is your fault you know' exclaimed Irene accusingly.

'Not now Irene' I responded. The last thing I needed was her nonsense while I tried to weigh up the options.

'If you could hold a job down for more than five minutes we wouldn't be in this predicament' she continued unabated.

'Perhaps if I wasn't running an unpaid care home and coffee house for the work-shy I wouldn't be in this predicament' I seethed.

'Daddy!' barked Ellen whilst giving me a stern look. I had overstepped the mark and made a mental note to refrain from such honesty in front of her again -although I couldn't guarantee anything where that was concerned.

'We need a plan of action' Irene turned to Ellen. I was apparently not capable of coming up with one in her eyes.

'I've got an idea' she replied. I was interested to hear this master plan.

'What is it dear?' enquired Irene.

'We move the car to a river, turn it upside down and take everything out then use it as a boat'.

'You – do as she says' ordered Irene whilst jabbing a gnarled finger in my direction.

'Brilliant. Yes I'll just get on and turn the car into a boat. Why didn't I think of that?'

'I'm just trying to help' remarked Ellen in a sorrowful tone. I put my arm around her.

'I know Ellen - I only wish it was that simple'. Irene looked at me disdainfully before then hauling herself off the verge and walking away like a sulking child. I hoped she had gone to play with the traffic.

'Do you think we'll get to Scotland?' asked Ellen with genuine hope in her voice.

'I don't know sweetie, the odds are stacked against it'

'You'll think of something – I know you can do it Daddy' she replied. It was the first time that someone other than Caitlin had shown any sort of faith in me and I was genuinely moved. She had unconditional belief in me even if it seemed a little misguided. My confidence and self-belief had fallen through the floor in the wake of the redundancy yet Ellen's unwavering trust went some way to restoring the diminished levels.

'Thanks Ellen, I'm working on it' I replied with a new wave of optimism.

'Will Nanny and I come into the interview with you?'

'I don't recall a pre-requisite to bring a child and pensioner in wedding attire with me' I joked.

'Who are those people in the van?'

'What van?'

'Talking to Nan over there' Ellen pointed towards a large dilapidated motor home that resembled something from a post apocalyptic movie. It was various shades of matte grey with customised panels and the odd partial red stripe – it was clearly in need of a good clean. I jumped to my feet and hastily approached the driver's window as Irene was engaged in conversation with the occupant. I wasn't sure what form of human would present itself from behind the wheel. In keeping with the vehicle's demeanour the driver sported the appearance of a futuristic renegade. He was wearing a bandana, beard, sunglasses and the remains of a well worn black leather jacket from which the sleeves had been ripped.

'Your wife tells me you need to get to Stirling' he stated with a gravelly voice.

'She's not my wife - I'm terribly sorry. Come on Irene' I couldn't believe anyone would think she was my wife. At that moment two other faces appeared at the open window behind the driver. They broke out into a chorus.

'Come on Irene
Oh, I swear what he means
At this moment - you mean everything
You in that dress
My thoughts I confess
Verge on dirty
Oh, come on Irene'

It was a perfect recital of 'Come on Eileen' and certainly broke the ice. We all laughed, even Irene who hadn't even smiled since the eighties. The driver extended an arm out of the window and we shook hands like men did, complete with the obligatory attempt to crush each others digits.

'I'm Razor, we're travelling up to Yorkshire – reckon you could use a lift. I would hate to think of Irene missing her big day'. The irony of his name wasn't lost on me, considering he was the proud owner of an unkempt beard that one could lose a badger in.

'I'm Tim, this is Ellen my daughter and I think you need no introduction for the other one'.

'It's cool man – get your stuff and we'll hit the road' he replied. It seemed anything but cool for me. Was I seriously about to embark upon a journey with a group of strange men whilst putting Ellen and Irene at risk? As we walked back to

157

the car I weighed up the options and the result was smaller than a list of England's football successes since the sixties. In short we had little choice. If we could get to Yorkshire then we had a good chance of making it to Stirling from there by some means as yet undetermined. Every hour was crucial and I reasoned that waiting around for another hour or two could be the difference between making the interview and missing it. If the mortgage was going to be paid then we simply had to get to Stirling. In any event – who in their right mind would pick up a hitch-hiking trio of our current make up? The decision was made and we gathered our possessions from Rachel's Polo.

'Daddy do you know those men?' enquired Ellen.

'Strictly speaking no' I could only answer truthfully.

'Then why are we getting in their vehicle?'

'You should only get into a vehicle with a stranger if your father is present'

'They didn't say anything about that when the policeman came to our school'

'They probably gave you the abridged version'

No, they didn't mention bridges either. Are you sure we should be doing this?'

'Don't worry it will be fine – trust me'

'This is going to be the best wedding ever' announced Irene.

'It is certainly going to be interesting – I will give you that' I responded. We made our way over to the decrepit motor home and Razor was at the grubby side door greeting us.

'Bring your stuff through and we'll put it at the back with the equipment'

'Sure thing' I said as we entered the vehicle. They say you should never judge a book by the cover and sadly on this occasion they were wrong. The inside matched the exterior - it was dark, dirty and dingy. It was surprisingly lengthy, sporting a seated area with kitchen facilities in the middle which I could see led through to more seating and storage at the rear. The other two occupants were sat playing cards at a makeshift table whilst smoking something that had the suspicious aroma of cannabis. A smoke haze decorated the air and hung as if suspended from the roof. I tried to not look horrified and then realised that I was making a much better job of it than Ellen. She looked absolutely mortified and at that moment I wondered again at what point this had become acceptable for me. We followed Razor to the back of the motorhome and there was a collection of dirty black guitar cases, a drum kit and speakers together with other band paraphernalia. I took comfort from this as I had always found musicians to be peace loving and unlikely to try anything underhand. I found my lungs drawing anxious breaths again as I surveyed our new mode of transport and remembered I had brought the beta blockers that David had given me to trial. If it continued I made a mental note to give them a whirl.

'I'm Mikey and this is Chris' announced the first of the inhabitants. Mikey was a scruffy individual who had last taken a bath many years ago based on the aroma emanating from him. Chris was a larger man with long curly hair tied back and a straggly goatee beard. He had slightly tanned skin – or was it dirt? I couldn't be sure and wasn't about to ask. Both were sporting denim waistcoats, tattoos and ripped jeans in keeping with the driver.

'So...I'm guessing you are in a band?'

'Yeah dude, we live on tour and just travel the country playing gigs. One day we'll hit the big time – I feel it. Right here' explained Chris pointing to his genitals for reasons best known to him.

'Cool – sounds great I really admire people who live their life doing what they enjoy'

'It's the dog's man. We party, get high, get laid, move on and repeat. What could be better than that?' interjected Mikey.

'Yes I'm struggling to come up with something at the moment' I replied. It sounded like the sort of abandonment and general hedonism that I could use right now. It occurred to me how different my life had been compared to these men, who had no responsibility or plan other than to enjoy themselves.

'So what's with Stirling?' asked Chris.

'Well it's a long story but basically I need to get to an interview that I hope will save me losing everything I've ever worked for'

'Wow that's bad shit. Do you want a toke on this?' offered Mikey as he held out his smoking cannabis joint. I looked down at Ellen.

'I don't really smoke'

'Too bad, what do you do?' asked Mikey

'My career and family take most of my time. I'm happy with that'

'Sorry Daddy but what career?' enquired Ellen.

'Yes good point I don't have one right now'

'Daddy worked in an office but they made him a redcurrant'. The guys laughed.

'Redundant Ellen'

'You're a slave to the corporate prison?' Mikey seemed surprised.

'Some might call it that. But it's given us a nice home'.

'Look where that got you. Now you've ended up doing the same as us' reasoned Mikey. He had a point. The fact our paths had crossed was more an indication of how desperate and immoral I had become in the quest to save our house.

'Listen I need to repay you in some way but I'm a bit short at the minute' I thought it best to be honest.

'That's fine dude we need someone to help us with the gig tonight'

'Okay...I can do that – if you're sure. I don't play'

'Don't worry there's no need for musical ability' he replied – a worrying indictment of the standard of their music.

'Well I'll look forward to that'

'We might need a hand with a few other things along the way man'.

'Sure, I'll do what I can to help' I replied whilst wondering what this might entail.

'I wouldn't trust a word he says if I were you' stated Irene. I thought she was talking to me about Mikey but alas no, she was warning the nomadic musician about me. We made ourselves as comfortable as possible in amongst the plethora of objects and general aromatic clutter in anticipation of the long road ahead. I gazed out of the window and wondered once more where my life was heading. Clearly this was more of a concern than I wanted to acknowledge or accept – my heart started racing and I felt short of breath at the thought of our current predicament. I remembered the anxiety pills that David had given me to trial and frantically started checking my pockets, but for some reason they weren't on my person. This in turn added to the feeling of discomfort and I was having difficulty regulating my breathing as the beginning of a full blown panic attack was beginning to take hold. I simply couldn't have a repeat of the kitchen incident in front of our new found friends – they would not understand. Of course the thought of the ensuing embarrassment made me feel even more anxious and it was becoming increasingly harder to disguise my rapid breathing and heightened edginess. I was starting to feel dizzy and disoriented.Irene reached down to her bag and unzipped the front pocket before reaching inside and rummaging around. Eventually she pulled out a blister pack of pills and waved them at me.

'Is this what you're looking for?' she asked. I felt like I'd won the lottery.

'Where did you get those?' I enquired.

'You dropped them when you were loading the car'

'Thank you Irene' I was genuinely grateful – a rare positive spike in our relationship to date. I wasn't sure of the strength of the tablets and reasoned that David wouldn't have allowed me to trial them if there were any associated risks. I popped two of them and felt them slip down my throat. It was more than likely a placebo effect but almost instantly I felt much calmer and the dizziness started to subside. Nobody apart from Irene had really noticed the terror and I felt confident the situation had been contained – the only person who was aware would forget in the next few minutes.

'Dude – we're gonna drive to the gig and then get some food after' announced Mikey.

'No problem we will fit in with you' I agreed – mainly as I wasn't in a position to object.

'When are you going to grow a pair Tim?' asked Irene.

'It will be bad news for you when I do' I countered. It wasn't a joke.

After a short while the beta blockers started to take effect and I felt a genuine sense of serenity – probably the most relaxed I'd felt for a long time. My phone vibrated furiously in my pocket – a cursory glance revealed it was the roofer. There was also another missed call from Richard Long. I was sick of him hounding me but decided he could wait a little longer while I tried to secure the job. Suddenly I didn't give a shit about him or the fact we were hurtling along the motorway in a decrepit mobile fleapit with three disparate lowlifes, copious amounts of illegal cannabis and an old age pensioner in a wedding dress. I should have been worried and certainly if not about that then maybe the fact Rachel's Polo had been left abandoned by the roadside. Not that she had even attempted to contact me. But my new found pills took all of the worry away – they were the perfect panacea and I felt able to deal with anything that life threw at me.

'Let me know if any of you need the toilet – we'll stop at the services' said Mikey.

'Thank you, I've just been though' replied Irene straight as an arrow.

'But...there's no toilet in the bus?' he advised looking worried. He had every right to be concerned and I knew his worst fears were not unfounded.

Highway to Hull

After four hours of traversing the motorway in our less than exotic mode of transport we finally reached the intended destination - a public house on the outskirts of a small village near Hull. We were halfway to Stirling and for the first time it seemed we may even reach our destination. A weather beaten sign hung limply outside and I could just about make out the name 'The Pink Flamingo'. Unfortunately the flamingo portrayed in the haggard painted sign had long since surrendered its pink hues in favour of a murky white. The pub itself was a nineteenth century building sporting what I could only assume to be the original windows – they were rotten. In fact the whole demeanour of the property was one of near dereliction and decay. However I decided to reserve any further judgement until we had at least set foot inside the place.

'This looks a right dump. Tom – can you start taking some of the equipment through to the area just left of the bar' scowled Razor as he strode purposefully along the length of the vehicle.

'It's Tim' I pointed out but it didn't seem to register. Ellen looked at me and smiled. I grabbed hold of the nearest object which was a dust filled amplifier and followed Razor and his cronies out of the vehicle into some much needed fresh air. Having been cooped up in the stale smoke infested motor home for hours I took the opportunity to replenish my lungs. It was the best inhalation I could remember. The fact that Razor perceived this place to be a veritable dump spoke volumes about the level of filth I could expect to encounter inside. Razor threw open the door and the local barbarians greeted us with the obligatory stare designed to ward off anyone from the outside world. I suspected the approval process to become accepted wasn't pretty and it certainly made my local seem much more appealing than it ever had before. A bearded man lurking behind the pumps motioned to Razor to take the equipment round the bar to a clear area on the left side that had been designated for such events as this. We trudged around the bar, past the local ogres and set the equipment down on the floor next to the stage.

'Whatever you do Tom, don't start any fights with this lot. They're a pack of wolves and you my friend are a small lamb. If it kicks off I can't promise you protection' he warned.

'Don't worry I tend not to make a habit of picking fights with large hairy ogres' I joked before turning round to find exactly the person I'd just described stood behind me. The goliath caused a partial eclipse with his large frame. More impressive was the commendable service his body performed of supporting his gargantuan belly. Years of poor food choices and an unholy amount of beer had taken its toll on this man.

'I'm Tim, nice to meet you. We're really looking forward to performing for your delight later' I offered my hand nervously to shake his.

'We don't like your kind in here' he replied looking right through my eyes and deep into my skull. I could feel my brain retreating to the far recesses of my head in order to escape this monster's gaze. Thankfully at this stage it was only his stare that penetrated my head, as opposed to his large fist. Glancing around the room it was apparent this was predominantly a place where unemployed fans of heavy metal music would congregate and chew the fat over pints of manly lager. Virtually everyone I could see fitted this demographic. Having never been a fan of such music I felt to all intents and purposes about as welcome as a tabby cat at a Rottweiler convention. I didn't want Ellen and Irene coming into this establishment under any circumstances. I still had no answer for the man who was blocking my exit.

'He's cool don't worry' advised Razor and I hoped his word was enough to convince this ape to back off and let me pass. After a pause of what seemed like forever he stepped aside and his unflinching glare continued as I exited the place to go and fetch more band equipment. At that point I would gladly have just kept walking but I felt indebted to Razor for helping us reach the heights of Preston in our quest for the unholy grail. Ellen peered out of the window as I approached the motor home. Mikey and Chris were carrying one of the large heavy speakers from the back of the vehicle and struggled towards the main entrance with it. I decided to concentrate on the easier to carry items. The beta blockers were wearing off now and I was aware the anxiety was beginning to rear its ugly head once more. My breathing had taken on a more restricted feel and mild pangs of dizziness were presenting themselves.

'Irene have you got another couple of those tablets?' I asked in the faint hope that she might remember who I was.

'You're addicted to them – I knew this would happen' she replied whilst fetching a blister pack from her bag. I hurriedly swallowed the pills and started retrieving more items from the motor home. Razor was now beside the vehicle waiting to board as I stepped down onto the gravel drive.

'Dude you better watch yourself with that guy, he's got it into his head you might be batting for the other team if you know what I mean'.

'What? That's ridiculous – for one thing I've got a daughter!' I blurted in response to this unexpected accusation.

'Do me a favour – don't talk like an office boy when you're in there. They hate all that corporate bullshit these guys are right into anti establishment stuff. Don't look anyone in the eye and keep your head down – best advice I can give you'.

'Oh fucking great – are you saying I might get a pasting for appearing to be something I'm not?' I asked in an exasperated tone.

'It's history dude – this shit happens all the time, you need to man up my friend'.

'Listen I think I might just wait in the motor home once it's all set up if that's alright with you?'

'I hope you're not reneging on your offer of help tonight. I don't take kindly to that sort of thing' his tone changed and I sensed he wasn't joking.

'No of course not – what do you want me to do?'

'It's simple – we are going to pump this place full of industrial heavy noise and I need you to use this angle grinder to cut the shit out of the metal props. It's a new idea we've had but we're all tied up with the music. It will really help us take things to a new height Tom – are you cool with that?'

'I've not used one of those before but I'll give it a go' I found myself saying. At that moment I became aware of a light headedness. I wasn't sure why and could only assume it was down to the beta blockers. We took the angle grinders and metal props into the pub where I did my best to avoid looking at the locals for fear of receiving a pummelling. I wished I could swap places with Irene – this was so far removed from my comfort zone it didn't even register in the same galaxy. A man was the sum of his experiences and I felt apprehensive about the latest one. The only way to approach it was from a positive standpoint. It was a real sink or swim scenario I felt.

After a short while the stage was set up and I left Razor and company to perform their sound checks. I wandered back to the motor home where Ellen and Irene were playing top trumps with a deck from Ellen's collection.

'Can we eat yet Daddy?'

'We will get some food once we've finished performing, they said we'll go shopping and get some petrol' I explained.

'Oh okay....I'm hungry that's all and so is Nan' she replied.

'Hopefully it won't be long before we can eat' I lied. I was starting to feel very peculiar indeed and the sensation was nothing like the earlier experience of the beta blockers. Although I didn't feel anxious I was seeing stars and there was an unexplained feeling in one particular area of my body.

'Irene can I have a look at those tablets?' I wanted to check the dosage was right or if there was a warning with regards to possible side effects.

'Here they are' she reached into her bag and passed the open pack to me.

'These look different to the ones I had earlier and there are only two missing?' I enquired tentatively.

'Oh you must have had these earlier then' she handed me a different blister pack with two beta blockers missing.

'So if I've only had two beta blockers then what the hell were those tablets you gave me a while ago? I was growing increasingly concerned by this point.

'Ah...they must be Eddie's tablets to help with his little problem' she looked apologetically at me.

'Irene – please don't tell me you've just given me what I've think you've given me' I was now experiencing a feeling of abject horror. I looked down at the blister pack and noted the dosage of a thousand milligrams per tablet.

'Oh my absolute god, these are extra strength and I've just taken two of them! What the hell were you thinking?!' I demanded. There was a distinct stirring in my loins and my worst fears were starting to be realised as I could feel the blood rushing to my genitals at a rate of knots. The effect of this meant it was taking blood away from areas that I needed it such as my head - not to mention my hands which were needed at any moment to demonstrate angle grinding to a baying crowd of morons.

'What am I going to do? You absolute idiot! You do realise people are only supposed to take one of these at the best of times? You've given me two high doses of the stuff!' I ranted whilst flailing my hands in Irene's general direction.

'Nan didn't mean to Daddy she was just trying to help'

offered Ellen by way of explanation.

'I know darling but without going into too much detail these tablets are not meant for me'. I was aware of a bulging below the waist and needed to get away from Ellen quickly as I didn't want her to notice the reaction these tablets had caused. Reeling from this development I stepped outside of the motor home into the evening air and there seemed to be considerably more stars than previously. How many of them were real I could only guess. I felt incredibly odd at this point as I stood there in the near dark with a rock in my trousers and weighed up the options available to me.

'You ready Tom? Come on dude everything is all set up and the crowd are getting restless – they want some industrial noise. Let's go' ordered Razor and put his arm round me as he practically frogmarched me towards the waiting pub. My mind raced but I couldn't think of any way out of this debacle. There was only one way I could think of nullifying the excited organ and so I made my excuses and headed straight for the toilets before the gig started. It was like a rock and I had never known anything like it. I stood there in the cubicle and tried my best to address the situation but due to the anxiety I was also feeling about the impending performance I was unable to finish to job in hand. It was not helped by Mikey then banging furiously on the cubicle door demanding I joined them immediately.

'Right I'm coming for fucks sake' I snapped and just about managed to pull the trouser zip over the swollen area. I followed Mikey through the busy pub and we climbed aboard the stage area. Razor shoved the angle grinder at me and was not best pleased judging by his demeanour. Then they proceeded to kick off the 'performance' with quite frankly the worst form of music I had ever experienced in my entire life. There seemed to be absolutely no structure to it – Mikey was wildly thrashing at his guitar and Razor was screeching like a lion with its testicles in red hot lava. Chris attacked his drums with absolutely no sense of rhythm and as far as I could tell this was an exercise independent to the rest of the performance. It was deafening and atrocious in equal measure. Then there was me, stood there with the biggest erection in the history of man whilst wielding an angle grinder and making so many sparks that thankfully nobody seemed to notice. To say this was a defining moment in my life was an understatement of gargantuan proportions. Once again if someone had told me I would be doing this a few months ago I would never have believed it, yet here I was. I could only hope that the large hairy ogre from earlier didn't spot my aroused state as he already thought I was 'batting for the other team' and this would do nothing to change his opinion as the room was full of men. To my surprise the crowd were absolutely lapping up the industrial noise that we were bouncing off the walls and for a brief moment I almost enjoyed the adulation from the previously hostile mob.

During the interval I very quickly ran to the gents and addressed the situation in hand. This provided temporary relief for all of fifteen minutes before the stirring resumed and it was back again in all its glory. As I ground metal like never before with the angle grinder it dawned on me that Irene had been the reason I was here in the first place. If she hadn't struck up conversation with Razor at the roadside our journey could have been very different. But then would I have changed it now if I could? The honest answer was no – although I felt part of me had died when I was made redundant part of me was very much alive.

Late Night Shopping

After the gig we gathered our equipment and shuffled out of the Pink Flamingo leaving its feral inhabitants behind to revel in the aftermath of the eardrum splitting nonsense we'd served them. My head felt like it had been detached and was orbiting the rest of my body, such was the effect of Irene's industrial strength pills. The worst part of it being their original intended use – my mind kept wandering to thoughts of this Eddie character and Irene - it didn't evoke the most pleasant imagery.

'You okay Tom?' asked Razor, who was carrying one of the enormous speakers on his shoulder as if it was weightless.

'I feel a little off colour – can we get some food once everything is packed?'

'Sure – I saw a potential place to eat on the way, just down the road'

'Anything' I replied whilst watching the stars and listening to the ringing in my ears. Ellen came running out of the motor home to greet me.

'Daddy we're hungry'

'Yes I expect you are, sorry it took longer than I thought. We're getting food in a moment don't worry' I reassured her. She ran back into the motor home presumably to impart this information to her incontinent grandmother. We proceeded to gather the remaining equipment and all piled into the decaying house on wheels before departing the scene of the musical crime we'd just committed. If I never saw the Pink Flamingo again it would be too soon. I could see silhouettes of its animated occupants through the bay windows as we made our exit and it gradually disappeared into the distance, hopefully forever. The swelling was finally starting to subside much to my relief but I sensed it would be some time before the accompanying fuzzy head passed. A dull headache was starting to gather momentum, presumably as the blood was being redistributed to areas that had been starved for the last few hours. I felt very tired and glancing at my watch realised it was actually quite late. The sun had given way to the moon and it was nearly eleven o'clock – I wasn't convinced many food vending establishments would be open at this time of night. After a while we pulled into a retail park and Razor dragged the cumbersome vehicle into a space around the side of a large super-market before parking up.

'Come on Tim it's time to go shopping' motioned Chris as he pointed in the general direction of the supermarket.

'Sure thing. Ladies you wait here, I'll get you what I can' I advised. Irene just looked at me in a distrusting way and Ellen was already half asleep at this point. We climbed down from the vehicle and back out into the crisp night air. It was starting to rain a little – not heavily but it was that fine rain that just seems to hang in the air, slowly soaking you in a stealth-like manner.

'Razor this supermarket doesn't look very open?' I pointed out whilst looking at the dark building sprawled out in front of me. As I surveyed the layout of the car park it was apparent that during the day only disabled people or parents could park anywhere near the building. I wasn't sure of the chances of thirty disabled customers all choosing to descend on the shop at the same time. It seemed a little strange to me.

'Which space does a disabled parent park in?' enquired Chris who was clearly thinking along the same lines. It was assumed this was a rhetorical question as nobody graced him with a response.

'So unless I'm mistaken this place is very much closed' I re-iterated as we approached.

'Enough with the negative bullshit' rasped Razor.

'We have a little job for you' announced Chris as he produced a crowbar. He then retrieved what looked like a balaclava and a bag from his backpack.

'Time to go shopping -you'll have about two minutes to grab as much as you can before the Scuffers arrive. We'll get you in, think of it as a kind of Supermarket Sweep' he instructed. I assumed 'Scuffer' was a colloquial name for the police.

'Very funny guys' I retorted assuming this to be a joke. It wasn't – they were deadly serious.

'You owe us man – now it's time to repay your debts' replied Razor. I didn't think it was a good time to suggest he spent some of the income from the gig on a takeaway for us all. Then it came to me in a moment of inspiration.

'Why are we breaking in when there's free food in the bins around the back?' I asked.

'We aint eating out of no bins' Chris stated. The irony of it amused me.

'The supermarkets literally put all the out of date stuff into the bins – everyone knows that.'

'No they don't – they give it to the homeless' Razor countered.

'That's what they tell people and yes it's true to a certain extent. It's just they let the homeless come to them. Come with me' I motioned to the gang to follow me as if I knew exactly where the bins were. As we marched around to the dimly lit area at the rear of the supermarket a selection of large Grundon bins came into view. I hoped they contained the bounty we were seeking otherwise the Supermarket Sweep was going to be a reality. I should've known their generosity was going to come at a price and possibly one that I didn't want to pay but we had limited options when we accepted a lift from them. The moon poked out from behind the veil of clouds and provided some welcome light on the subject. I strode confidently towards the first bin and threw open the heavier than expected lid. As the heavy duty plastic crashed into the back of the supermarket building the moonlight revealed a collection of black plastic bags nestled together inside the bin.

'Dude that looks like rubbish to me' stated Chris.

'And it smells like rubbish' added Razor. I decided to ignore their collective pessimism and began opening the other bin lids and my hopes started to fade as each bin produced another bounty of waste. As I went to open the last bin I had another of the all too familiar moments where I questioned the direction my life had taken. If someone had told me the events of the last few weeks were on the cards I would never have believed them. It made me wonder what lay ahead in the world of Tim Fellows. I hadn't even prepared for my interview tomorrow and at this point it wasn't even clear if I would even arrive in time for it. But I had to do whatever it took to get there as I had sold myself the dream that this job was the solution to my problems. By the light of the moon I threw open the last bin lid in front of the watching morons. To my absolute relief this bin contained a selection of packaged food – there were sandwiches, ready meals, vegetables and all manner of consumables.

'Gentlemen, the Tim Fellows Self Service Restaurant is open for business' I announced.

'You are bloody kidding me!' declared Razor looking genuinely surprised. They moved in like a pack of starving hyenas that had chanced upon a meaty carcass on the African plains. The guys piled into the large industrial bin and were wildly removing food packages whilst practically salivating in the process. The bag soon bulged with food and they began filling their pockets and arms with as much as they could gather. The only sight I could recall that came as close to this in terms of desperation was the moment our local supermarket brought out a trolley of reduced items on a Sunday afternoon. A crowd of customers who had been waiting in anticipation would frenziedly dive in at once. Their faces would be contorted with a disturbing food lust as they fought with each other to save twenty pence off a packet of

173

pork loins that they probably didn't even want. This event occurred every Sunday around three o'clock and was becoming a bit of a spectator sport. I was pleased at my moment of inspired thinking as we headed back to the motor home with our newly acquired sustenance. Although it was free and had been removed from a bin it was a much better alternative than committing a crime and the outcome was the same. We boarded the motor home, Ellen and Irene perked up when they saw the banquet that was about to be consumed.

'Nice one Tim – you have more than repaid your debt. We will be eating free for many a night ahead – who would've thought they just leave all this food in the bins?' announced Chris.

'Well as I said – they are giving it to the homeless just not directly'. I explained as we tore open a variety of food packages like starving foxes.

'So we're eating food that was meant for homeless people?' asked Ellen. In that moment the realisation hit home that my attempt to avoid becoming the perpetrator of a crime had unwittingly robbed many homeless people of their future meals. I wondered what had happened to my moral judgement since the redundancy as I took a bite out of a particularly delicious sausage roll.

'I know how it looks Ellen but I have been making a monthly charitable donation out of my salary to the homeless many for years' was all I could manage by way of justification.

'So now you're just taking something back' laughed Razor although the humour wasn't shared. Irene shook her head and gave me one of her looks. I was grateful for once that her short term memory was deteriorating as she would've enjoyed relaying this to Rachel at the dinner table before sitting back to enjoy the ensuing fireworks. I wondered what kind of impression I was making on Ellen more importantly. In the last 24 hours I had taught her it was okay to abandon cars by the roadside, accept lifts from strangers and steal food from the homeless. She was of course unaware that my choice in respect of the food consisted of either becoming a criminal or a coward and the latter was marginally more acceptable in the circumstances. I longed once more for the stability and security of a regular job, although I had no idea where Rachel's thoughts lay or indeed my own in terms of the family unit. Never before had there existed such uncertainty in my world, it was very disconcerting. I could feel the anxiety building again and tried not to think too deeply as it wasn't helping.

After our veritable feast we again resumed our journey and I seemed to have been upgraded to hero status in the eyes of our new found cohorts. Irene snored loudly and Ellen was sound asleep as I stared out of the filthy window at the silhouetted tree tops as they passed by. I felt shattered but all the excitement had left me in the throes of an adrenaline rush that prevented the onset of sleep. I made a pact with myself to resume my charity payments to the homeless once I found a new job in order to recompense them for having sold them down the river. I felt ashamed that it was Ellen who had provided the insight into the flawed decision I'd made – it really hadn't occurred to me at the time, I was just relieved that I didn't have to perform the supermarket sweep. It was hard to work out where we were in the country but all I knew was that we were edging closer to Scotland and that could only be a good thing. The motor home left the motorway and we journeyed along a smaller network of roads for a while until Razor eventually brought the vehicle to a halt, presumably so he too could sleep. That however was not the reason – he appeared in the half light of the rear quarters, his frame taking up a fair amount of the available space in the aperture between the middle and rear of the vehicle.

'We need to get some more fuel and quickly – the tank is below the empty' he announced. Chris and Mikey were soon on their feet and the three of them were now stood facing us.

'Sorry are you requiring my help with this?' I asked, wondering what was now occurring.

'Everyone needs to help. Follow me' instructed Razor as he opened the side door and he stepped out into the night closely followed by the others – including Irene in her wedding dress. I grabbed Ellen's hand and we disembarked the motor home. It took a moment for my eyes to adjust to the darkness and I couldn't quite make out where the others were. As my vision improved it became apparent we were in a wooded area next to the roadside and there appeared to be a collection of small buildings set back from the road.

'Sorry Razor I thought you said we needed fuel? Are we walking to the garage?' I enquired.

'Who said anything about a garage?' he responded. I was starting to get the distinct impression we were about to break the law again and a pervasive feeling of dread swept over me.

'I'm not sure I follow?'

'It's simple – we're going over there and borrowing some fuel from those cars' he explained whilst pointing in the direction of the small buildings. There were a few rows of waist high hedgerows that seemed to form some sort of mini maze around the border of the small hamlet. As I looked a little more closely at the development it then became clear that these small buildings were in fact not buildings at all. They were caravans and mobile homes.

'Oh please tell me you are joking? You are absolutely insane if you think I'm going over there and stealing fuel from those travellers. I'm sorry but this ends right here – we're done' I ranted in an uncharacteristic outburst.

'You need us to get to Stirling – what other plan have you got? Anyway if it wasn't for you we wouldn't be this far up the country – we're doing you a favour man and this is how you repay us? Now you want to just walk away and leave us stranded in the middle of nowhere?' he barked. Chris and Mikey moved closer to Razor and hunched their shoulders in a show of solidarity.

'Look – you said I'd repaid my debt so why are you now asking me to steal from gypsies?'

'You repaid your debt up to that point. But now we've taken a detour to get you to Scotland so you can at least put some fuel in the tank' Razor countered.

'When did we agree this? You said you would take us as far as you could and that was all'.

'Oh just go and get the fuel Mr Poopy Pants – don't you know I'm freezing my bits off out here' chided Irene.

'Mister who?' If I'd had false teeth they would've been on the woodland floor by now.

'If you had a pair we wouldn't be in this mess now. You let my daughter get away with murder for years and now we're all here paying the price' she snapped.

'So now you think this is my fault? I suppose you think the redundancy was my fault too! Anyway, the apple doesn't fall far from the tree Irene that's all I'm going to say' I retorted in a rage. How dare she start pinning the blame on me – she had no idea of the sacrifices we'd made to accommodate her. It seemed a bit rich to attribute her daughter's shortcomings to me especially as she was the one who had provided the moral guidance in her formative years.

'Daddy and Nanny stop arguing!' pleaded Ellen.

'I'll show you who is Mr Poopy Pants around here – come on Razor lets fill up' I ordered in an authoritative tone. All sense of judgement had dispersed and with my male pride wounded I did what most men would do and tried to prove my masculinity.

'Finally....now you take these' instructed Mikey who handed me a pair of large plastic water carriers that looked like they were army issue.

'Now we need to be deadly quiet guys. Follow me and keep close to the ground as this lot cut up rough in a tear up'

'Sorry can I have the English translation for that please?' I asked.

'They will give you a proper bunch of fives Corporate Boy'

replied Mikey. I really was starting to feel like a fish out of water and no amount of corporate speak was going to cut the mustard with the travellers if they caught us. We crept along the inside edge of the hedgerows and advanced closer to the parked caravans. Our only guide was the light afforded by the moon and as my bravado subsided it gave way to a sense of trepidation. I had no idea where in the country we might be and here we were about to borrow fuel from the travelling community. Could my life take any more crazy twists I wondered? Razor motioned to Ellen and Irene to wait by the hedgerows as we quietly sneaked towards the nearest vehicle which was attached to a fairly sizeable caravan. Mikey carefully twisted the fuel cap on the elderly Audi and produced a short length of flexible hose pipe.

'Suck on this until just before the diesel hits your mouth' he whispered, handing the pipe to me.

'What? You want me to do it?' I whispered back in exasperation.

'Come on Poopy Pants just get on with it' Chris responded grinning away to himself. The other two sniggered at his quip. It had the desired response – I took the hose pipe and pushed it into the fuel opening and pushed it down into the depths of the tank. Then I sucked as hard as I could and after a couple of attempts ended up with a mouthful of diesel. It was honestly the most disgusting taste since Rachel last attempted cooking, which was quite some time ago. It took all of my willpower to keep the noise to a minimum as I spat the excess fluid onto the crisp grass. The others tried again to contain their amusement. Chris pushed the loose end of the hose into the first canister and the diesel flowed slowly along the tube and audibly into the container. A little too audibly for my liking if the truth was told. After what seemed like an eternity the first canister was filled and I took it over to Irene and Ellen, swapping it for the second one. All we needed to do was to repeat the process and then leave this place. I could then be assured of safe passage to Stirling and the all-important interview. It sounded simple as we began filling the second container and my confidence that we could actually carry out this audacious mission had begun to increase. Suddenly the silence of the night was shattered by a loud cry.

'Oi!!! Get away from that car!!' came the shout from an indeterminable source and with that we all leapt to our feet and began to run like headless chickens towards the hedgerow. I was aware of more voices and lights being deployed behind me as we hurtled towards the hedges. The others were hurdling over the waist high hedges and I performed my own version which included stumbling and falling over them. There seemed to be many more than I recalled seeing when we first arrived. For some reason Chris and Mikey were laughing as they clambered over them – they were actually enjoying the thrill of the chase! I glanced back and could see the figure of the shouting man as he too hurdled over the privet hedges in hot pursuit. It was strangely quite an exhilarating experience but at the same time absolutely terrifying. I wasn't sure where I found the athleticism from to evade capture and could only assume the fear of reprisal from the gypsy folk was the driving force. I had read about people finding previously undiscovered reserves of strength when faced with fight or flight situations. I was now on the flat ground and could see the motor home ahead of me in the darkness. As I ran towards it I realised I had lost sight of Ellen and Irene in the melee. I hoped to Jesus they were on board the decrepit vehicle. I leapt onto the motor home and Chris was just ahead of me.

'Chris where are the girls?'

'Not on here mate – we need to go' he replied whilst breathing heavily. My heart was beating so hard I thought it was going to combust.

'I can't leave them' I replied instinctively. The motor home had started up and was beginning to move.

'Then you better go find them' he answered emphatically, shoving me in the chest. I fell backwards and out of the motor home onto the woodland floor. I watched as the vehicle then sped off into the distance with our few belongings. I couldn't believe what I was seeing -there was no honour amongst thieves it seemed, I was absolutely stunned as I sat there trying to recover my breath in the crisp night air. Then a firm grip presented itself on my left shoulder and I realised that I was out of the proverbial frying pan but about to be thrown into the furnace.

A Decent Proposal

After being frogmarched back towards the traveller settlement by my captor I was taken to one of the mobile homes and virtually thrown in the front door. The interior was surprisingly well furnished and clean, I wasn't sure what to expect but this completely challenged any preconceptions that I may have garnered over the years.

'Daddy!' Ellen shrieked and came running over to me with outstretched arms. It was such a relief to see her and I couldn't believe that I'd lost her in that moment of primal fear. I wasn't so worried about Irene if the truth be told.

'Hello Darling I'm so sorry we got separated. Are you okay?'

'Yes I'm fine. Nan is next door with the beardy man'. I was aware of a gathering of others inside the home and until now my priority had been Ellen. Casting my eyes around the room I observed a couple of henchmen and a weathered gentleman who I assumed to be their leader. He was sat in a leather armchair and his lady was perched in an adjoining chair. He looked like the sort of person you wouldn't wish to upset and right at this moment he was faced with me – someone who had been stealing fuel from his camp.

'Tell me, what brings the likes of you to this part of the world?' he asked with a guttural voice. I was unsure how to answer this and what the right thing would be to say.

'Hello I'm Tim- it's a bit of a long story to be completely honest with you'.

'I'm the kind of person that likes their sleep and when I am woken in the night it had better be for a good reason' he replied in a measured manner that still implied violence was just a hairs breadth away.

'Of course Sir I totally understand and completely share your frustration' I started to stammer.

'This isn't a fucking call centre. I'm waiting for you to explain yourself man. Save the customer service crap for someone else'. Of course he was right and the various training sessions I'd attended down the years strangely didn't cater for the situation I now found myself in. I noticed the presence of a gun on a small table and this added to the feeling of anxiety that was sweeping in like severe weather on the Welsh coastline.

'Of course, I'm sorry. The truth is we are trying to get to Stirling and were given a lift by the guys who just drove off. They made us help them steal the fuel but we didn't want to. They said they would leave us here in the woods if we didn't do it'

'What sort of a man runs and leaves his wife and child in the company of strangers?' he asked.

'This really isn't my thing I'm not going to lie. Not long ago I had a steady job and would normally be asleep at this hour. For one reason or another I now find myself in the strangest of places doing things I wouldn't have ever considered. All thanks to the bloody banking system and their failure to lend responsibly. Honestly we mean you no harm' I decided to blame a third party and one that I hoped they took exception to as well.

'Yes the banks have screwed everyone over good and proper. I don't trust them, never have and never will' he agreed, much to my relief. I still sensed we were some way from finding a way out of this predicament but at least we had established a mutual dislike of the financial institutions that had caused the recession. He started to chuckle to himself and turned to look at his partner and she in turn began to laugh. The henchmen also started to laugh but none of them seemed too sure what they were laughing at.

'Do you know Tim in all my years nobody has dared to try

182

and steal anything from our site. Then when it finally happens it's a corporate drone, his wife and child!' He laughed much more heartily now and the others joined in.

'She's not my wife' I felt compelled to explain. The room fell silent and the laughter ceased.

'Then why is she in that dress and what's with Stirling?' he asked gruffly. At that moment the door burst open and Irene appeared with her arm interlocked with a portly bald man sporting a goatee beard and an array of tattoos.

'The Doc has agreed to take us to my wedding in Stirling!' she shrieked. I was about to instinctively remind her there was no wedding but then it dawned on me that this situation could work to our advantage.

'That's very good of you' I announced reaching an outstretched hand towards the man known simply as Doc. He looked me up and down but didn't return the handshake. Instead I looked at my watch as if that was what I originally intended to do. Not that anyone was fooled although Ellen giggled to herself.

'How long will it take to get to Stirling?' I enquired.

'You're looking at around six hours' he replied in a thick Yorkshire accent.

'Six hours? Is it really that long by car?' I was astonished as we were already a fair way up the country to the best of my knowledge.

'Takes a couple of hours by car' he replied.

'But you just said six hours sorry?'

'Have you brought a car?'

'No'

'Then we go by horse and trap' he explained. I tried not to look disappointed as my frazzled brain processed this latest information. If they thought I was going to an interview the chances of them still taking us were remote. This Doc gentleman had for some reason taken a shine to Irene and it made sense to use this to our advantage. So long as everyone thought we were going to a wedding then we had our passport to freedom.

'That really is very kind of you, I can't thank you enough' I said.

'I'm getting married tomorrow!' exclaimed Irene as she then began a bizarre jig around the room in her wedding dress. Doc took her arm and they both performed a dance that loosely resembled Irish folk dancing as the rest of the room clapped in unison. The whole dynamic had lifted and there was much merriment in the air as we celebrated Irene's fictional wedding. After a while of celebrating and bonding it was agreed we should get some sleep before the long journey in the morning. Doc had explained we needed to leave at 6am in order to get to the church in Stirling for midday, which was the time Irene told him she was getting married. It was already two o'clock in the morning by the time we went to bed. As I lay in the bed provided I once again took stock of the latest development and hoped this was the last hurdle to overcome before the interview. If we could get to Stirling for midday it would give me enough time to purchase another suit from a charity shop and freshen up. It was the only plan I had at this juncture and there was still everything to play for as the saying went. I found it hard to sleep with the adrenaline still coursing around my tired frame but eventually everything went black and the dream factory opened for business again.

The dreams were a mixed bag, starting with me having been shrunk and walking aimlessly through the metropolis as the city skyscrapers towered over me menacingly. Then I was in a room full of dogs that were talking before they noticed me and started barking wildly before launching an attack, during which I managed to scramble towards a trapdoor which I then fell through onto the deck of a boat. This vessel was being chartered by some sort of rogue pirate who was dressed in a topcoat and tails. I asked him where we were headed and he explained he had some special cargo below the deck. Walking down the rickety steps I found myself in a room with various display cabinets. Each one had a plaque inside and an object. Leaning closer the first one was labelled 'Tim's Mouse' and there was a stuffed harvest mouse mounted on a plinth inside. Then another labelled 'Rachel's Mug' and inside was a ceramic mug with a picture of me on the side. The cabinet labelled 'Tim's Career' was empty. There were pictures of Caitlin and Ellen scattered around the room. Thinking it all a bit strange I ventured back onto the deck to remonstrate with the pirate but he had vanished and Irene was now at the helm.

'Irene what are you doing?' I asked as the wind and rain howled right through us.

'Someone has to get this ship back on course' she shouted, giving the wheel an almighty turn just as a bolt of lightning lit up the stormy sky. I awoke in a sweat and that was the end of my night's sleep.

In the morning we were able to use the washing facilities provided by our hosts. The fact that washing facilities existed at all dispelled another myth in my mind. It all seemed so surreal, whilst I didn't doubt for a minute they could mete out punishment on a whim they were also very courteous and hospitable to us during our stay. It had once again fallen to Irene to inadvertently save our bacon and as much as I reasoned that she had landed us here in the first place, it didn't really matter in the cold light of day. The main thing was that Stirling was now in our sights and we were but a horse ride away. The sun had risen quickly and a misty haze hung over the valley that we seemed to be in. I thought of Razor and how his gang had discarded us without a second thought. But then what else could I have expected from a gang of renegades who were living off the grid, scavenging and stealing whatever they needed in between performing the worst music known to mankind.

'Are you ready Daddy?' Ellen asked from the front door.

'Yes I'm good to go'

'Doc has got the horse ready, I can't wait!' she exclaimed excitedly. All of this was a bit of an adventure for her and also

185

for me. I followed her out and the bearded Doc was waiting outside. He led us around the park and we came to a clearing where a handful of piebald horses were tethered. Steam could be seen rising from their flared nostrils in the cold morning air as they became excited at the sight of the four of us.

'This one's a good 'un' he advised has he began to untie the horse and started applying some sort of harness and other paraphernalia to the animal.

'What's she called?' asked Ellen.

'We call her Rocket on account of her speed' he explained, giving a wry smile. Irene was surprisingly subdued as we watched him prepare the horse and carriage. After a short while we climbed on board, Irene sat at the front with Doc and we clambered into the seats at the rear. I hoped it wasn't going to rain as none of us were dressed for inclement weather. Doc gave the reigns a swift tug and we trotted out of the encampment and onto the main road to a chorus of whistles and cheers from a few of the residents. I had never envisaged journeying to my all important interview on a traveller's horse and trap under the pretence we were attending Irene's wedding. I just hoped Irene's memory didn't result in her telling Doc another story that conflicted with the wedding ruse at any point over the next six hours.

The horse it transpired was named Rocket as an ironic nod to her lack of speed. She chugged away unflinchingly but at a relatively slow speed. The seats at the rear were less than comfortable and we felt every single bump or crack in the road surface. Not only that, but it looked to all intents and purposes that we were heading to a gypsy wedding. This attracted all manner of staring, hand gestures and comments from car drivers who each thought they were the first to do so. After several hours of it I was fed up with seeing 'the look' from each new driver who was forced to follow us until it was safe enough to pass us by.

'Not long until we reach Stirling' announced Doc after

several hours. It was approaching midday and he was under the illusion we needed to be there for that specific hour.

'That's brilliant thank you' I replied.

'Time is a bit tight so I'll drop you at the church'

'Oh there's really no need, anywhere in the town is fine'

'No I insist – I can't bear the thought of Irene being late on her big day' he patted her on the knee affectionately. She smiled back at him like a love struck teenager and I had to look away for fear of becoming ill. I looked at my phone which for once had a decent enough signal to allow me to research the church address in Stirling. There was one at the top of a hill near the high street and I hoped our ruse wasn't going to be uncovered upon arrival there. My phone displayed missed calls from Caitlin and Richard Long but nothing from Rachel. I wondered where she was or if she'd even noticed we were gone.

We arrived at Stirling and the sun was high in the sky, it was a glorious day and the streets were alive with shoppers and tourists soaking up the atmosphere that the day offered. The town was set on a hillside and as we rose towards the top of the high street I could see the Wallace Monument in the distance behind us. It looked imposing and intriguing at the same time, a nod to the past in respect of a prominent figure in Scotland's fight for independence. I could see a church appearing ahead and there was actually a wedding progress. Guests had gathered around the entrance and thankfully there was no sign of the real bride to arouse suspicion. Doc pulled the horse and trap to a halt outside and the onlookers stared in total disbelief at the four of us. I had become so accustomed to it now that it barely registered.

'Thank you so much Doc you have been an absolute star' I said, shaking his hand vigorously. I meant every word.

'No trouble son, you're sister deserves the best' he informed me as he winked at her. I helped her down and hoped he would then start his long journey home. He didn't. A few of the legitimate wedding guests were looking at us in disbelief but we just had to ignore them and keep up the pretence as we started walking down the path towards the large double doors of the church. We glanced behind us again and Doc was still at the gates waving us on.

'Is he seriously not going to leave?' I remarked to Ellen and Irene.

'Are you here for the wedding?' asked an usher at the door.

'Yes, sorry about her she likes to wear her dress on such occasions' I advised motioning to them that she was a sandwich short.

'That's fine come with me Sir' he said as he wheeled around and took us inside the church. We gave a last wave to Doc and hoped he would disappear.

'Which side are you on?' asked the usher. I had no idea whose wedding we were at.

'It's fine we know where we're sitting' piped up Irene nonchalantly. Sometimes I had to admit to myself she could be very useful but it was only now that this had become apparent. In my hour of need the person who had come through for me was Irene. People still had the ability to surprise me and that was something that made life interesting. My life had descended into one big bucket of filth since the redundancy and the future was an unknown quantity yet this woman who I had resented for years had somehow shown me the path to follow when my own judgement was on its knees. I felt bad for the way I had treated her with contempt all this time. This whole experience had been very humbling and it was only when your back was against the wall that you realised who was looking out for you and who wasn't. Sadly Rachel fell into the latter category and recent events had served to highlight our incompatibility. When I really thought about it I knew we weren't suited and spending time with Caitlin had highlighted the gulf between us. I needed to know if Rachel felt the same. The chances were that if one person was unhappy so was the other.

We took our seats near the back of the church and I was aware of people looking over at us and then conferring before shrugging their shoulders. I gave the occasional nod and this seemed to work. With Irene in the wedding dress we weren't exactly inconspicuous. All we needed to do was wait for a moment or two just to allow for Doc to leave. I hoped he wasn't planning on waiting outside for too long or it would put us under pressure to get to the interview in time. Suddenly it became apparent the actual bride had arrived and the traditional music began as she was led along the aisle by her proud father and the tears began their descent from the eyes of many an onlooker. It brought back memories of my own wedding and I hoped the groom received more support from his wife to be in the coming years than I had. The large wooden doors were closed behind the bride and her entourage and we were now trapped at the wedding of complete strangers. I glanced at my watch and the sands of time were starting to slip through our fingers. The vicar began his speech and my mind wandered to more pressing matters until he reached the only interesting bit.

'If anyone knows of any reason why these two cannot be married-'

The double doors had been opened and there in the bright light stood the silhouette of a man. Everyone looked around at this new entrant and there was a tangible anticipation in the air.

'If I don't say this now I'll regret it forever' the stranger announced as he strode towards the bride and groom. Then the horrific realisation dawned on us – it was Doc. He thought the bride was Irene and was making purposeful strides towards the altar to deliver his case.

'Jesus Christ we've got to get out of here' I spluttered to Irene and Ellen.

'I love a bit of wedding drama can we stay?' begged Irene, who had clearly forgotten who Doc was.

'Trust me Irene we really need to get out of here right

now with the minimum of fuss if we're going to meet Fred in time' I lied.

'Oh yes we mustn't be late' she agreed, co-operating for once. We quickly took our chance and made for the doors while everyone's attention was fixed firmly on Doc who was about to make a monumental fool of himself. As we left I could hear him asking where Irene was. We hurriedly dashed along the exit path and I took the first turning I could find. It brought us onto a raised path that seemed to circulate around the perimeter of the hilly town, roughly half way up. We could see across the land for miles and the view was breathtaking. The sun served to enhance the various shades of green and a group of golfers indulged in a few rounds on the sprawling course below us.

'Why do you always spoil my fun?' asked Irene.

'Irene I need you to trust me on this one please' I replied as I tried to gather my breath.

'It's been an exciting adventure Daddy I can't wait to tell everyone' chirped Ellen.

'Well it's probably best that we keep this as a special memory between us. They are the best ones' I replied whilst praying to the god that I didn't believe in. There was nothing that had happened over the last two days that I would want broadcasted. If Ellen imparted any of the events to her school I would end up with a visit from Social Services. In reality if I was honest it had all been an adventure and I would never have experienced any of it had I still been gainfully employed. Sometimes things happened for a reason and I had been living in a rut for such a long time that I hadn't even noticed. Maybe I was meant to realise there was more to life. Ellen walked over to the viewpoint and gazed out onto the rolling fields and meadows below. Just for that moment it seemed as if time had stood still while we gathered our thoughts and our breath.

'I feel like I've let everyone down Irene' I confessed. I didn't know why I was telling her but there was something cathartic about being able to unload my troubles on someone who wouldn't remember. It was a win-win situation for everyone.

'That daughter of yours thinks the world of you Tim. She was filling out the front page of that book you bought her for Christmas, answering questions about her life. Do you know who she put down as her hero?'

'That cartoon guy with the big white body?'

'No, she put Daddy' explained Irene. I was taken aback by this revelation as I thought I had been nobody's hero of late. I felt my eyes well up for the first time in many years and looked away so that Irene didn't see. Ellen performed cartwheels against the backdrop of the sunlit fields and blue sky, the gentle breeze rustled the leaves of the trees around us and the world suddenly seemed a better place to be, if only momentarily.

'When you get home, do what's right for you Tim and nobody else. You know what I mean. I don't know how you've put up with Rachel for all these years' she said knowingly. Maybe she had been more aware of the marital disharmony than she let on. I knew there were big decisions to be made and they would have to follow once we returned home.

'Thank you Irene, for everything' I responded after a short while. I genuinely meant it and put my arm around her. She looked at me with eyes that told a thousand stories but said nothing in return.

'Daddy it's nearly two o'clock we need to get to your interview' announced Ellen, breaking the moment and injecting a sense of urgency into proceedings.

'Christ yes – let's get moving! I hope I can find a suit in the charity shops and quickly!' I stated as we got to our feet and started to follow the path around the edge of town. I hoped we wouldn't encounter Doc again in the town centre.

We rushed around the streets of Stirling in the early

191

afternoon sun, trawling the wares that were on offer at a variety of charity shops. Luckily I had found a shirt, tie and shoes quickly so it was just the suit remaining. The clock ticked ever faster as we headed towards the last shop and my hopes rested squarely on its shoulders. It amazed me how many times I'd seen these suits in charity shops recently but now I actually wanted one they were scarce. We raced into the shop and I began rifling through the collection of suits hanging amongst the small collection of men's clothing tucked away in the corner.

'Are you looking for something in particular dear?' enquired a voice from behind the counter.

'Not really' I responded as I feared she would just slow me down.

'He's looking for a suit to wear to an interview' Ellen interjected. It was apparent there were none that would fit. I gave her a look as I didn't think we had time to engage in chit-chat with the locals.

'I think we've had another one come in, it's out the back' the lady behind the counter explained.

'Oh really? Could I see that if at all possible?' I asked hopefully. She disappeared into the mysterious room at the back and I could hear her rifling through bags. After a couple of minutes she came back and brandished a full diver's suit.

'Right...I was under the impression you were looking for a suit for me?'

'Well you didn't specify which kind of suit. These are the most popular that we sell' she rebuked. I looked around the shop - there were no other diver's suits for sale. Clearly this woman was a little odd.

'Okay my apologies for the oversight. Do you by any chance have any men's work suits ideally with a chest size of forty four inches and waist of thirty four?'

'I do like your dress madam. Are you getting married today?' the lady asked Irene, without even acknowledging my request.

'Yes Dear I'm marrying Fred' she replied as if it was

192

actually happening.

'There's nothing like young love' the cashier joked. Irene laughed along with her.

'We could show these youngsters a thing or two don't you know' remarked Irene giving me a wink.

'I married my Bernie in fifty four. It was a beautiful day, the doves were singing and the children were dancing, it was magical. Bernie had a drop too much to drink mind you and I wasn't best pleased when we got back to the hotel room' the cashier went on to say.

'Hello? I'm sorry to interrupt this trip down memory lane but I really need to get to this interview at three o'clock' I interjected before it carried on any longer.

'Today?' asked the surprised cashier.

'Yes I'm afraid so. As you can see it's now half past two and I still don't have a suit'.

'Well you'd better not be hanging around here chatting to the likes of me then young man. Off you go and good luck' she replied. I tried my best to hide the frustration but it wasn't easy.

'Thank you and good day' I sarcastically remarked as we turned to leave. I pulled open the front door and just at that moment the cashier called out.

'I have a suit out the back'

'This isn't another swim suit is it?' I asked cautiously, not wanting to waste any more time. She disappeared and then finally emerged from the depths of the sorting room with a nice modern suit. I hoped to God it was the right size and had already decided if it wasn't I would shoehorn myself into it regardless.

'Thank you! I'm just going to try it on' I took the suit gratefully and rushed to the changing room which was basically a cubicle with a dark purple curtain across the front. I pulled the heavy curtain aside and a lady shrieked from inside the cubicle.

'Oh my God I'm so sorry! I wasn't thinking' I tried to explain and quickly replaced the curtain to the closed position. I could hear the occupant muttering words of complaint from behind the curtain.

'You can use the store room' the cashier said. I dashed in there and tried the suit on – to my absolute relief it fitted although there was room for a bit of growth. To save time I put on the shirt, tie, shoes and suit and then performed a quick glance up and down the mirror before heading back out into the shop.

'That looks great Daddy!' Ellen stated. She seemed very pleased. I approached the cashier and retrieved my wallet from my crumpled trousers in the bag.

'How much is the suit?'

'It hasn't been priced up'

'I know that, how much would it be if you did price it up?' I could see the clock ticking and was starting to become very concerned as the interview was a good five minute walk from our current position.

'Seven pounds and sixty six pence'

'Okay here's ten pounds' I gave her the crumpled note.

'Do you have the odd two pounds and sixty six pence?' she asked. I wondered why nobody wanted to give change any more, it had become an obsession that shop keepers must keep hold of their loose change and only deal in notes.

'I'm afraid I don't'. She huffed and puffed as she counted the change out as slowly as was humanly possible before handing it over.

'Good luck young man' she offered.

'Thank you for your help' I replied and we finally left the shop. Although I felt I had edged much closer to Irene's age in those few minutes it was a huge relief to finally be dressed in business attire. We spilled out onto the street and walked down to a point where the road split in two. The street bustled and the sun was still magnificent in the sky.

'Ellen I would like you to take your Nan to that library over there and wait for me. Whatever you do please don't talk to any strangers and make sure she doesn't leave. Can I ask you to do that for me?'

'Yes of course we will be fine. I'll read Nan a story' Ellen said excitedly.

'Both of you, I really appreciate your help over the last couple of days. I just want to be successful and make you proud of me' I explained honestly.

'But you are a success Daddy' Ellen replied with unswerving conviction and in that moment it felt like something had clicked in my addled brain. None of this really mattered to Ellen – she didn't care if I was a Chief Executive Officer of a blue chip company or a traffic warden. She thought I was a success regardless and I realised in that instant as we stood in the sunlit street in Stirling that she was right. I had become so obsessed with trying to get back onto the corporate ladder that I had lost sight of the things that were important. I had even changed my feelings about Irene and that was something I never thought would happen. I was only too aware that after the interview it was uncertain what kind of reaction I would return to but as long as the people who really meant something were there – I needed nothing else. I counted Caitlin in that category.

'Thank you Ellen, that means a lot to your old Dad. Do you know something -if I don't get this job then it's fine so long as I have such a great daughter as you' I stated, straight from the heart. When I reflected on how people had said that redundancy was second only to bereavement I had my doubts. Having experienced it for myself now I could honestly say it was the worst thing that had ever happened to me. In hindsight though- I wouldn't have changed it for the world.

I arrived at the interview with seconds to spare and the receptionist showed me to the seating area as I waited for Mike Townsend to come down from the lofty heights of his office. The building was modern and I felt immediately at home despite the fact I would rarely need to visit the place if I secured the job. The lift doors opened and a gentleman in a sharp blue suit strode towards me with an outstretched hand.

'You must be Tim?' he had a firm grip.

'The one and only' I quipped.

'Sorry to have kept you, we've started using this new system and it's causing a few headaches. Have you heard of Paradox?'

'It's funny you should say that — you're looking at the expert' I advised, feeling like the proverbial phoenix.

'Excellent! How was your journey?' he enquired.

'I feel like I've come a long way' I replied.

30868044R00112

Printed in Poland
by Amazon Fulfillment
Poland Sp. z o.o., Wrocław